sence of

Mine Enemies

Other Books by Debbie Viguié

Tex Ravencroft

The Tears of Poseidon
The Brotherhood of Lies
The Lords of Atlantis (Summer 2018)

The Kiss Trilogy

Kiss of Night
Kiss of Death
Kiss of Revenge

Sweet Seasons

The Summer of Cotton Candy
The Fall of Candy Corn
The Winter of Candy Canes
The Spring of Candy Apples
The Summer of Rice Candy (Spring 2018)

Witch Hunt

The Thirteenth Sacrifice
The Last Grave
Circle of Blood

Abracadabra

Now You See Me
The Lady Vanishes (Winter 2019)

In the Presence of Mine Enemies

Psalm 23 Mysteries

By Debbie Viguié

Published by Big Pink Bow

In the Presence of Mine Enemies

Published by Big Pink Bow

www.bigpinkbow.com

Dedicated to Curryanne Hostetler. Thank you for everything.

Thank you to all the fans, friends, and family who support and encourage me to keep doing what I'm doing. Thanks especially to everyone at the Debbie Viguie Book Club Facebook group for making me laugh a lot and reminding me why I do this.

1

Detective Mark Walters usually liked Sundays. They were the one day of the week that he was almost always off and got to spend time with his wife and children. This Sunday, though, was turning into a nightmare that he kept praying he would wake up from.

Detective Keenan had stormed into Joseph's house with half a dozen uniformed officers and arrested Jeremiah for murder. Whose murder, Mark was still unclear on. The whole thing was preposterous, and he couldn't believe that Keenan had been keeping him in the dark on whatever investigation he thought ended with Jeremiah.

While Joseph called his attorney, Mark decided to head to the precinct and see if he couldn't find out more about what was going on. Hopefully his presence there would also serve to keep Jeremiah from going berserk on them. Mark had seen the rabbi's eyes when the officers were trying to handcuff him. Only Cindy had been able to get through to him in that moment. It was a good thing she had, or they might be adding murder of police officers to the charges.

After letting Geanie know where he was going Mark left as fast as he could. As he drove down the hill that Joseph's house was on, he couldn't help but wish that if this had to happen that it could have happened at a different time. Cindy's brother, Kyle, and their parents had witnessed the whole thing. Given that Kyle and Carol already disliked Jeremiah, things couldn't be much worse on that front.

Mark's heart was pounding, and he realized that he couldn't be more scared if he'd been the one arrested instead. He had no idea what Jeremiah would do if pushed. Or, rather, he had a good idea and that's what scared him. Without knowing who the victim was he also had no idea if it was someone Jeremiah had actually killed or not.

"I need a vacation," he muttered after he blew through a red light and almost got sideswiped by another car.

Right before the cops had come for Jeremiah, the secret organization that they'd been trying to take down members of had contacted Joseph. They wanted him to join. That was its whole own mess. If he sent Joseph in undercover he could get hurt or killed. If Joseph declined he could still get hurt or killed since the organization seemed very invested in maintaining its secrecy. With all that going on he needed the rabbi on the streets, free to act. He couldn't have him in prison or under Detective Keenan's microscope.

"God, we need a lot of help," the words came tumbling out of him. It was the closest thing to a prayer that he'd ever uttered, and he meant every word of it.

A powder blue car turned onto the street right in front of him and he had to slam on his brakes to keep from hitting it. He fishtailed slightly before stopping safely. He flipped on his lights and siren and shot over into the next lane. He raced by the offending vehicle and the driver didn't even have the sense to pull to the side.

By the time he had skidded into a parking spot at the police station his nerves were completely shot. He raced inside and headed straight for his captain's office. The man's door was open, and Mark bolted inside.

"Captain, I-" he stopped in mid-sentence as he realized that Detective Keenan was already there. Before he could stop himself he yelled, "What the hell was that back there?"

"I was just doing my job," Keenan retorted.

"That's a load of crap. You stormed that place with half a dozen officers like you were expecting trouble, and you didn't even have the courtesy to give me a heads up about what was going down."

"I don't owe you anything. This is my case, not yours, and you are not my partner or my supervisor. If you don't stand down, I'll arrest you for obstruction of justice."

"If you don't show me some respect then you can arrest me for assault and battery against a police officer," Mark growled.

"You think you can take me?" Keenan sneered.

"I know I can."

"Bring it!"

A loud whistle pierced the air. The Captain stood up and glared at both of them. "Mind if I have a say here?"

Mark hunched his shoulders and stared down at the ground. Keenan fell silent as well.

"Listen up, idiots. I want this as neat and clean as possible. Keenan, you've arrested a man who is not only an upstanding member of the community but also someone who has personally helped us out on numerous occasions. I want you to be rock solid with your facts before you go any farther. Mark, if you can't stow your personal feelings then you are out of here until this is sorted out."

"Sir," Keenan said. "Given his friendship with the accused, I don't believe there's any way Mark can stow his feelings and be objective."

Mark looked up quickly. "Sir, with all due respect, the detective here has wantonly overlooked his single best asset when it comes to getting inside the head of the accused. Yes, the rabbi is a friend, but if he murdered someone in cold blood without provocation, there should be consequences," Mark said, trying to choose his words carefully. It was especially important to do so given how angry he was. He didn't need to inadvertently give Keenan more ammunition against Jeremiah. "Frankly, I think Keenan is overzealous because the rabbi helped solve a case he couldn't, clearing the name of a wrongly accused man."

"I don't need civilians to help me do my job!" Keenan shouted, turning red in the face.

"All evidence to the contrary," Mark said, struggling to keep from raising his voice as well.

A knock on the door caused them all to turn. Liam was standing there, an uncertain look on his face. "You sent for me, sir?" Liam asked.

"Yes, come in," the captain said.

Liam glanced from Mark to Keenan and slowly entered the room.

"Gentleman, I think the entire department can agree that Detective O'Neill here is our resident boy scout."

"That's true," Mark said, wondering what was about to happen.

"No arguments here," Kennan said.

"I figured this situation had the potential to blow up in my face, in all of our faces, if things aren't done right," the captain said. "That's where Detective O'Neill comes in."

Mark looked at Keenan. The other man looked as confused as he was.

"Detective O'Neill, you've had the opportunity to work with Rabbi Silverman?"

"I have," Liam said.

"He stands accused by Detective Keenan of murder. Detective Walters claims he's innocent. Both men are going to be doing their darndest to prove they're right. Do you follow?"

"Yes, sir."

"I want you to oversee both detectives in this process. Ultimately, it's your best judgment that I'm going to rely on. And I expect you to render *your* best judgment. Am I clear?"

Liam took a deep breath. "Crystal, sir."

Mark measured his next words carefully. "Sir, given the circumstances, it's clear that what Detective Keenan has is only circumstantial at this point."

"That's for Liam to judge."

"Okay. Detective Keenan has yet to reveal the name of the person he thinks Rabbi Silverman has murdered. In fact, I know, since I was present, that Detective Keenan declined to tell Rabbi Silverman the name at the time of his arrest."

The captain looked sharply at Detective Keenan. "Is that true?"

"Given the circumstances I felt it would be unsafe to discuss the matter in detail with bystanders present," Keenan said.

Mark seethed. "I disagree with the detective's assessment of the situation," he said.

"How can you until you know the facts?" Keenan asked.

Mark felt a twinge of panic. Keenan knew something, something real. He needed to find out what it was and quickly, so he could do his best to spin this.

"I think now is an appropriate time to illuminate Detective Walters," the captain said.

"Not unless he surrenders his weapon first," Keenan said.

"Captain, I'm a patient man," Mark said.

"No, you're not," Liam rebutted.

Mark turned to glare at his partner.

Liam shrugged. "I will use my best judgment to determine the truth."

At that moment Mark wasn't sure who he wanted to punch more: Kennan or Liam. He turned back to the captain. "Captain, what in the hell is going on?"

The man took a deep breath and held out a hand. "Give me your gun."

Mark told himself that shooting all three men would get him nothing. He slowly pulled his gun free from its holster and handed it to the captain. "You want my badge, too?"

"No, this is just a safety precaution," he said, putting the gun in a drawer. He turned and nodded to Keenan who closed the door and then leaned up against it.

Mark felt completely trapped. He looked at Liam. "Do you know what this is about?"

Liam shook his head.

"Mark, as a fellow cop, I'm asking you to sit down," the captain said, his voice suddenly soft.

That frightened Mark more than anything that had happened in the last hour. In fact, he hadn't been this terrified since he thought that Traci was going to die giving birth to their twins.

"I think I'll stand," he said, his voice sounding hoarse to him. His mouth had gone completely dry.

"Then, as your captain, I'm ordering you to sit down."

Mark did as he was told. His hands were beginning to shake, and he folded his arms across his chest in order to hide them.

Keenan cleared his throat. "Jeremiah Silverman is the chief suspect in three unsolved murders."

Three.

Mark's heart began to race. One was going to be hard enough to find a way out of, but three? He just prayed they were murders Jeremiah hadn't actually committed.

"Who?"

"Peter Wallace. He was found dead on the rabbi's lawn."

It took Mark a second but then he remembered. "The homeless guy?"

"Yes."

Relief surged through Mark. Jeremiah had told him that he hadn't killed Peter, but that he wasn't sure who did. They could catch the real killer, and everything would be fine.

"Just because he found the body on his property doesn't mean anything. The man was stabbed a couple of blocks away."

"There is evidence that points to Jeremiah having known the man," Keenan said. "And more."

"He didn't do it," Mark maintained.

7

"He's also the chief suspect in the murder of a foreign national at the wedding of Joseph Coulter."

Mark did his best not to flinch. That particular foreign national had been a terrorist and Jeremiah had killed him.

"He didn't kill him," Mark said. "I was there. I know."

"Your job at the moment is not to counter the evidence. There will be time for that later," the captain said quietly.

Mark sighed and nodded.

"He's also the chief suspect in the murder of Benjamin Hughes."

Mark wracked his brain but couldn't figure out who that was. That had to be a good thing. "Who is that?" he asked.

"The pastor at First Shepherd church. He was murdered last night."

Mark's heart skipped a beat. "What? I didn't hear about that."

"You're hearing about it now," Keenan said.

"Wait, last night? We were all at Joseph's. Jeremiah was there all night. We all were."

"But not all of you were awake all night. The rabbi left the house and killed the pastor."

"Why on earth would he do that?"

"Because they had a heated exchange over something very dear to the rabbi's heart."

"Oh?" Mark asked, still trying to figure out why Jeremiah could possibly be a suspect in the murder.

"Cindy. The pastor and Jeremiah had it out because the pastor disapproved of their impending marriage."

"That's no reason to kill a guy," Mark said.

"I agree," Keenan said, "apparently Jeremiah disagreed."

Mark shook his head and looked at the captain. "This is preposterous. These are all completely circumstantial and there's no way Jeremiah is guilty."

Well, at least not in two of the cases, he thought.

"Those cases are all ongoing investigations," the captain said.

"And I will find the evidence that links him to those murders," Keenan said.

Mark turned back to him. "I don't get it. This makes him a person of interest. You don't have enough to arrest him for any of those."

"You're right, I don't," Keenan admitted. "Not yet."

"Then why?" Mark asked, starting to stand.

"Mark, stay seated," his captain cautioned.

"We did have enough evidence to arrest him for a fourth murder."

"Please, entertain me, this just keeps getting better and better," Mark said sarcastically. He was trying to calm himself down and rattle Keenan at the same time.

"Rabbi Silverman killed a man who was digging into his past, who knew that he was not exactly what he appeared to be. When he got too close the rabbi executed him."

"And you think you have proof of that?" Mark asked, his brain working on trying to figure it all out.

"I know I do."

"Well?" Mark asked impatiently.

Keenan glanced at the captain.

"Go ahead," the man said.

Keenan nodded. "I have proof that Jeremiah Silverman murdered Detective Paul Dryer."

2

Mark lunged out of his chair toward Keenan, intent on strangling the life out of him. Liam grabbed him and tried to hold him back.

"That is not funny!" Mark screamed at the top of his lungs.

"Mark, calm down!" Liam pleaded, straining to keep hold of him.

Mark felt more hands on him and realized that the captain was trying to hold him back, too.

"Let me at that lying son-of-"

"Detective! Stand down!" the captain roared.

"You take that back!" Mark shouted at Keenan who had his hands up, ready to defend himself.

Mark lunged harder, and managed to get a few inches closer. "You can't get away with saying that!"

"Mark! Mark! Calm down!"

Mark stopped struggling. He couldn't shake off both men. After a couple of seconds, they let go of him. He leaped forward and punched Keenan in the face. The other man hit back and they both fell onto the ground.

"You take that back!" Mark demanded as he tried to pin his opponent to the floor.

Keenan kneed him hard, but Mark managed to keep hold of him despite the pain. They thrashed around, each trying to get the upper hand.

Suddenly pain coursed through his body and he spasmed as electricity hit him. The pain finally ended, and he flipped onto his back.

"Who tased me?" he demanded, looking up at Liam and the captain. Each of them was holding a taser in their hand.

"Whichever one didn't tase me," Keenan groaned.

"Don't make me lock you both up until you cool down," the captain threatened.

Lying there on the ground the shock really started to settle in and Mark began to shake from head to toe. "It can't be true," he whispered. But there was a sick, wrenching sensation in his gut that worried him.

~

"It can't be true," Cindy said, horror washing over her.

Joseph nodded. He had just gotten off the phone with Sylvia, the church's business manager. "It is. Pastor Ben was killed last night."

"That's terrible," Geanie said, tears glistening in her eyes. "I didn't like him very much, but I never would have wished that on anyone."

Joseph put his arms around her. "I know," he said, the emotion strong in his voice.

Cindy felt like she was walking through a nightmare. She turned and looked at her father who had a grim look on his face.

"She's calling an emergency meeting with the board and the staff in an hour at the church," Joseph said.

"This can't be happening," Cindy muttered.

She didn't have time for an emergency church meeting no matter what was going on. She needed to figure out a way to get Jeremiah out of trouble. She'd promised Mark she would sit tight for a few minutes until he could figure out what was going on. Well, she'd been sitting tight for quite a few minutes and there still had been no word from him.

"I need to go to the police station," she said out loud.

"I'll drive you," her father offered. "The rest of you can deal with the church thing."

"Thank you," she said softly.

Her father nodded.

Geanie put a hand on her arm. "They're going to need you. We're going to need you."

"I know, but Jeremiah needs me, too."

"Come as soon as you can," Joseph said.

Cindy nodded as she was suddenly afraid to speak lest she start crying.

~

Jeremiah felt like a trapped animal. He didn't like the feeling, and he was trying to keep himself calm so he didn't show everyone in the precinct just how savage he could be. He had been in much worse situations before but never as a civilian. He had a very limited number of options if he wanted to keep Jeremiah Silverman as a viable persona and life for himself.

He felt so bad for Cindy, especially that this had happened in front of her parents and brother. It wasn't fair. She deserved things to go smoothly for her, especially given everything she'd been through recently.

He'd been sitting by himself in an interrogation room now for about an hour. He didn't think it was a fear tactic the police were trying to use. Rather he suspected that Mark was raising hell and that was what was taking the police so long to send a man in to question him.

He began to breathe deeply and evenly, ensuring that more oxygen got to his brain so that he could think faster, more clearly. There could be no mistakes now. The next twenty-four hours would be the worst and he needed to be ready for anything that they could throw at him.

He glanced up at the camera in the corner of the room. He could be observed easily through it and he kept that in mind as he did his best to appear calm and collected.

Detective Keenan had not told him the name of the person he was being accused of murdering. That seemed odd to him. It could be that this whole thing was one big fishing expedition. The fact that they hadn't booked him could lend itself to that theory. The other possibility was that they were waiting for a particular moment to spring the name on him, hoping to elicit a specific reaction.

Whoever they named he was prepared to remain stoic. There was a long list of people he'd killed in the last few years, but with most of those he'd covered his tracks thoroughly. The best-case scenario was that this was someone he hadn't killed that they thought they could tie him to.

The door finally opened, and Mark walked in. He looked like he'd seen a ghost. He was pale, and he was sweating. A lump was forming over his right eye and the knuckles on both hands were scuffed up.

"Were you in a fight?" Jeremiah asked.

"As a matter of fact, yes."

"Did you win?"

"Fight was called on account of interference by fellow officers," Mark said.

Mark glared at the camera and then sat down stiffly at the table, his back to it. "I asked to be allowed to tell you what's going on before Keenan comes in here and interrogates you," he said.

"Okay," Jeremiah said, focusing on keeping his expression neutral.

"Keenan suspects you of killing three people and claims to have evidence that you killed a fourth."

"You and I both know that's ludicrous," Jeremiah said.

"Of course we know that, but he's got a bee in his bonnet. He thinks you killed that homeless guy you found on your lawn and a guy at Joseph and Geanie's wedding."

"Of course I didn't," Jeremiah lied. While he had not killed the first one he most certainly had killed the second one.

"I know, but I just have to tell you what he thinks. The other two are going to be a bit more of a shock," Mark warned.

Jeremiah took notice. Mark was trying to prepare him so that his reactions wouldn't give anything away. He wasn't sure what could be more upsetting, but clearly Mark thought it was going to be.

Mark took a deep breath. "Last night the pastor at Cindy's church was murdered."

"What?" Jeremiah asked, not having to fake the surprised reaction. "When? How?"

"Detective Keenan will be discussing that with you in a few minutes," Mark said grimly.

Jeremiah shook his head. "That's terrible, and I don't know why on earth he'd think I had something to do with it. Besides, I was at Joseph's house all last night along with everyone else."

"Detective Keenan will discuss his theory with you," Mark reiterated.

Jeremiah had several conflicting feelings. While he had deeply disliked the man and been angry with him for hurting Cindy. he'd had no intention of harming him. He couldn't believe what Cindy and the rest of the church staff were going to have to go through as they dealt not only with their own shock and grief but also with the shock and grief of the entire congregation.

"If there is anything the synagogue can do to help out, we'll be glad to," he said, meaning every word. "They're going to need to call in grief counselors right away to take care of the staff and the parishioners. Then-"

Mark held up a hand to stop him. "Other people are going to have to figure that out and deal with it. Right now, you have much more urgent concerns."

"The mental and spiritual well-being of my congregation and my fiancée's congregation are my most urgent concern," Jeremiah said, allowing his anger and frustration to show. "I need to help them."

"I respect that. You know I do. But first you have to help yourself," Mark said.

Jeremiah took a deep breath. "Whatever I have to do so I can get back to my job."

"Okay. Now, the detective believes he has evidence proving you killed one other person."

"Who?" Jeremiah asked.

Mark locked eyes with him and in his eyes Jeremiah saw fear and anger and something else, something furtive. *Doubt. He thinks it could be true*, Jeremiah realized.

"Paul Dryer."

Jeremiah stared at him. "Is this a joke?" he asked.

"I wish it was," Mark said.

"I didn't kill him."

"Keenan says he can prove you did."

Jeremiah leaned forward. "Mark, tell me you *know* I didn't do this."

Mark dropped his eyes. "I know you didn't do this."

Jeremiah grabbed his shoulder. "Mark, look me in the eyes and tell me that."

Mark looked up and there was so much guilt on his face that Jeremiah felt like a knife was twisting in his gut. Mark started to turn toward the camera.

"No! Look at me, not the camera. Tell me," Jeremiah said.

If Mark believed that Jeremiah had killed Paul then they had a problem too big for the two of them to be able to fix together.

Mark cleared his throat. "I know you didn't do this, but I'm not the one you have to convince."

Mark was lying, but there was nothing Jeremiah could do about it at that point. Pushing farther would just serve to underscore Mark's doubts about him which was ammunition he did not need to give to Keenan.

"Keenan already thinks I'm guilty. I doubt I'll be able to convince him of anything."

"That's true. That's why the captain has appointed someone to oversee this whole debacle and to decide whether or not there's enough evidence to send this to trial."

"Who?"

"Liam,' Mark said grimly.

Mark's partner and a friend. That should have made things easier but from Mark's expression Jeremiah could tell that it didn't.

"Don't worry, Mark. It's all going to work out just fine," Jeremiah said reassuringly.

"How do you know?" Mark whispered.

"Simple. I'm innocent." Jeremiah said firmly.

Mark nodded and then got up. "I have to let him come in here now and ask you questions. I'm sorry."

Jeremiah shook his head. "Don't be sorry. The sooner he asks the sooner I can get home."

It's what an innocent rabbi with nothing to hide would have said. Jeremiah even managed to give Mark a slight smile as he tried to sell it.

The door opened, and Mark left as Detective Keenan came in. The detective sat down across from Jeremiah. He had a stack of folders in his hands. He was also sporting a nasty cut on his cheek and some bruising around his throat. It was pretty clear he had been the one Mark got into a fight with.

"I don't understand what's happening here," Jeremiah said, putting enough worry into his voice to sound like a bewildered, innocent man.

"Sure you do," Keenan said bluntly. "You're being charged with murder and I know Mark already filled you in on the who."

"It makes no sense. I had nothing to do with any of those," Jeremiah said, running his hands anxiously through his hair.

"Cut the crap. We both know better," Keenan said.

"No, we don't. I don't understand how any of this is happening. I'm a rabbi. I help people. I don't hurt them.

And right now, you're keeping me from doing my job and helping my fiancée to do hers. A lot of people in the faith community are going to be grieving and scared. A serial killer targeted them a couple of years ago and a lot of people are just now getting over that."

Keenan leaned forward, his eyes boring into Jeremiah's as though trying to pierce his soul.

Jeremiah stared back, revealing nothing while trying to see exactly what was going on in Keenan's mind. The man believed what he was saying, that much he could tell. He thought he was justified in his actions.

"I know everything," Keenan said.

"Then please enlighten me," Jeremiah said, trying not to be combative in his tone.

"Paul Dryer was investigating you before he died. When he died his open cases came to me. The more I read his notes on you the more I knew he was right about something."

"What?" Jeremiah asked.

"Your name isn't Jeremiah Silverman and you're no rabbi."

3

"How are you holding up?" Cindy's father asked her once they were in the car.

"Not well," she admitted.

"I'm sure it's all just a misunderstanding," he said.

She looked over at him. "What if it's not? I mean, what if we can't clear him?"

"Then you have some decisions to make, and I suggest you make them together," he said.

"I can't lose him."

"You haven't yet, so stop acting like it. Let's assume the best and work to make it happen. After all, I just found a partner for cards and I'm not ready to give that up without a fight."

She didn't know whether to smile or cry at that. She was touched that her dad was being so supportive.

"Jeremiah's a fighter," he said.

"That's very true," she muttered.

"And if I had to guess I'd say he's been in worse spots than this and without the love and support he has now."

"Thanks for trying to make me feel better."

"I'm simply pointing out the facts," he said. "How's your arm?"

"Throbbing," she admitted.

"How long has it been since you took pain medication?"

"I don't remember."

"We'll get something in you as soon as we can."

She nodded. She wished the pain in her broken arm would distract her from the terrible fear building within her, but it didn't. The fear was consuming everything. Cindy was grateful that her dad was driving. It was all she could do to give him directions. Had she been driving she was sure she would have run every red light if only because she was too distracted to notice.

When they parked at the police station she took a moment to gather her wits and strength. Her dad reached out and grabbed her hand, giving it a squeeze.

"I'm right here with you," he said.

She nodded.

They got out of the car and headed inside. They had only gone about a dozen steps into the building when Mark spotted them and quickly headed over. He looked banged up and agitated.

"What happened to you?" Cindy asked.

"Fight with another officer," he said as though it were no big deal. "I'm not sure you should be here."

"Jeremiah's here so this is exactly where I should be," Cindy said, straightening her shoulders.

She noticed that there was some fresh blood seeping through Mark's shirt. "I think you might have opened your wound up," she said.

He looked down and swore. "I'll deal with it in a minute." Mark stepped close and dropped his voice. "We need to all be especially careful what we say and do. Keenan is loaded for bear and the captain has put Liam in charge of deciding whether he has enough evidence against Jeremiah."

"Liam's a friend," Cindy said, feeling a ray of hope.

"He is, but first and foremost he's a cop and he tends to walk the straight and narrow. That's why the captain picked him for this."

"I want to see Jeremiah," Cindy said.

Mark winced. "He's being interrogated now. You won't be able to see him for a while and maybe not then. You should just go home, pray, do what you do."

Cindy glared at Mark. "The pastor of my church was murdered last night. Sylvia just called an emergency meeting of staff and board members. I'm not there. I'm here, and I'm not leaving until I see Jeremiah."

"Look, I'm really sorry about Ben." Mark took a deep breath then lowered his voice even more. "And frankly, if you want to help Jeremiah the best thing you can do right now is prove that he had nothing to do with Ben's murder."

Cindy felt her heart skip a beat. "Ben? That's who they think he killed?"

"Among others," Mark muttered.

Fear raced through her. "How many others?"

Mark glanced around and then shook his head. "Not here."

"It's absurd. Jeremiah was at Joseph's last night. We all were."

"Can you swear he was there all night and never left?"

She blinked. "Well, no, but he would never kill Ben."

"The man who hurt you and tried to thwart your marriage?"

Cindy shook her head. "Never. And they don't have to believe me. Joseph has a million security cameras. I'm sure that they'll show that no one left the mansion last night."

"Except they don't."

"What do you mean?"

"I'm just now getting caught up to speed, but apparently last night the security cameras were off for two hours."

"What?" Cindy asked, shock rippling through her.

"I don't know what's going on, but I need your help. Jeremiah needs it."

Cindy nodded slowly. "I'll go and see what I can find out. Where was he killed?"

"At his home. The scene's been cleared but Keenan won't take it kindly if he finds out you were trespassing."

And suddenly Cindy was smiling. "It's a good thing I know the man who owns the house."

~

Jeremiah stared at Detective Keenan. "I have no idea what you're implying. I am Rabbi Silverman. I've been a rabbi for years. I don't know who else you think I'd be."

"As it turns out Paul Dryer knew quite a lot about pretending to be someone he wasn't. And he was on to you early on. He knew there was more to you than met the eye and he documented every encounter, looking for clues, chinks in your armor."

"I know that he didn't like it that Cindy and I were involved in investigations, but we had no control over that," Jeremiah said. "He never expressed any other concern."

"Of course he didn't, not to you, although I would be surprised if he never mentioned it to Mark."

"A man with a guilty conscience and secrets like Paul had, often becomes paranoid and thinks everyone is hiding something. I've seen that before in counseling people,"

Jeremiah said. "I feel sorry for him, knowing now the burden he was carrying."

"You feared him. That's why you seized your opportunity and killed him at Green Pastures."

Jeremiah shook his head. "He came up, trying to help us, and was murdered by the assassins that were hunting those of us trapped there by the flooding." He paused and glanced down. When he looked back up he was blinking back tears and there was a tremor in his voice. "I saw him get killed and I'll never forget how terrible it was."

"You buried him."

"It was all I could do for him. It was a gesture of respect and friendship. He came up there trying to save the lives of those kids and to save me. His sacrifice was overwhelming. We Jews believe that a body needs to be buried as soon as possible. I didn't know if I was going to make it out alive to tell anyone where he was or what happened to him. I buried him as I would have wanted someone to do for me. And, as soon as the kids and I were rescued, I told the authorities exactly where he was so they could move the body and reinter it somewhere more appropriate."

Jeremiah wiped the tears off his cheeks. He had learned years before how to cry on command. The tears were genuine, though. He still felt grief when he thought of Paul and the terrible way he had died. No matter who he was and what secrets he was hiding in the end he had given his life for others. No greater sacrifice could be asked of any man.

Keenan leaned forward, looking like a shark getting ready to attack. "Paul was killed by a Barrett sniper rifle. It's not something you come across outside of the military

23

much. So, imagine my surprise when we searched your house this morning and we found one."

"What?" Jeremiah asked, not needing to feign surprise.

"That's right. How do you explain that?"

"I can't. It's not mine. I have no idea how it got there."

"You expect me to believe that?"

"Yes, actually. If I'm the monster you think I am do you think I'd be stupid enough to leave a murder weapon like that just laying around my house?"

"Guys that are used to getting away with everything get cocky and eventually they slip up."

Jeremiah shook his head. "Given that last week you wrongly accused a man who was being framed for murder don't you think it's possible it could happen again? For all we know this is all still connected to that mess."

"No!" Keenan snapped.

Jeremiah knew he'd gotten under the man's skin. The detective wasn't one hundred percent confident that someone wasn't also trying to frame him and that it could even be connected to the case he had so thoroughly botched. A case where he had categorically rejected his and Cindy's help before they solved it anyway.

"I don't blame you for getting things wrong. On paper I'm sure that Leo looked guilty. Don't let your own guilt over that push you to do something now."

Keenan stood up so quickly he knocked his chair over.

"This is not guilt or retaliation!"

There was a knock on the door a moment later and Keenan turned bright red. Mark walked in. "The captain wants to see you."

"We're not done here," Keenan snapped at Jeremiah before storming out.

"You really think antagonizing him is the way to go?" Mark asked.

"I'm not trying to antagonize him. I'm just trying to point out some facts and demonstrate that he might be operating under a strong set of emotions that are clouding his judgment."

Mark rolled his eyes, but didn't comment. Instead he said, "Cindy and her father came here to see you."

Jeremiah felt like a knife was twisting in his gut. "How is she?" he asked.

"Upset. But she is a woman with a mission. She's going to solve Ben's murder."

"Good. How was Don?"

"Supportive. Lucky for you."

"Yeah, I'm feeling really lucky," Jeremiah muttered.

~

Cindy had the strongest feeling of déjà vu as she walked into her old house. "Thanks, Harold," she told her former landlord.

"I hope you find whoever did this," he said, shaking his head. "I don't know what the world is coming to that things like this happen."

"I know," she said. "You're the one who found him?"

"Yes. He didn't show up this morning for church and he wasn't answering the house phone or his cell so several of us became concerned. I came in and… well, he was dead in the bedroom," Harold said, choking up.

Cindy put a hand on his arm. "I'm so sorry you had to go through that," she said.

Harold wiped his eyes. "I'll never forget the look on his face and his eyes were just… empty."

She understood more than most and her heart broke for him. "Was the front door locked when you got here?"

He shook his head. "It was unlocked. That made me suspicious."

"Was there anything else you noticed before finding him?"

Harold shook his head and wiped his eyes again.

"If you need to talk, I'm here," she said.

He nodded. "If you don't mind, I don't want to go in again. Just give me a call when you're done, and I'll come lock up."

"Thank you," she said.

Harold left, pulling the door closed behind him. Don pulled two sets of disposable gloves out of his pocket and they put them on. Don had to help her because of her broken arm.

"Why is it every place I've lived it seems bad things happen?" she asked.

"Are you up for this?" Don asked.

She pulled herself together. She couldn't fall apart. There was far too much on the line. It was just hard not to flashback to the things that had happened in this house when she had lived there. "Yes. You?"

"There's a first time for everything," her father said with a wry smile.

"Thanks for coming with me."

"Wouldn't miss my chance to see my amazing daughter solve a crime in person."

She hugged him. "Thank you," she whispered.

"I have two amazing children and one of them doesn't get nearly enough credit."

"That means a lot."

She let go of him and cleared her throat. "Okay. Let's catch a killer."

They moved toward the bedroom. They both paused for a moment on the threshold and then stepped in.

Cindy sucked in her breath sharply. It was like stepping back through time. The furniture was all there, just as it had been when she lived in the house. The knick-knacks were different, but the space was familiar.

She grabbed hold of the dresser, grateful that she was wearing gloves. The biggest difference in the room was not the knick-knacks but the blood stain in the middle of the bed. In her mind she could see Ben lying there dead. She had been told that he had been stabbed and she couldn't help but think about the dead man she had tripped over in the church a few years earlier. That had happened back when this was her house and her bed.

She remembered her fear when an intruder had broken into her home to search it, looking for the Shepherd's cross that he had lost at the scene of the crime. She also remembered Jeremiah going through her house to make sure there was no one in it when he had driven her home. She never would have guessed then where the two of them would have ended up. They had solved so many mysteries together and become each other's world in the process.

"You okay?" Don asked.

"Flashbacks," she said.

He nodded as if that were the most natural thing in the world.

"No evidence that there was a struggle, so he was likely asleep when he was stabbed," Don said.

"Harold said his eyes were open."

"Even if he was stabbed in the heart there would have been shock and a second where his eyes opened."

"That is really awful," Cindy said.

"Agreed. Did he have any enemies?"

"None that I know of, but he'd been the pastor at First Shepherd for less than a year and I don't know much about his life before he got here."

"Harold said the front door was unlocked."

"Someone must have picked the lock."

"Unless he was the type who never locked his door," Don said.

Cindy shook her head. "I remember hearing him warn a new parishioner who was from the Midwest that while Pine Springs was a safe town, they still needed to make sure they locked their doors at night. We should doublecheck the windows, though. We want to make sure the killer didn't come in that way and then just leave out the front door."

They checked all the windows, but they were all locked from the inside. The second bedroom looked like it was being used for an office, which was just what Cindy had done with the space as well. What her father had asked about Ben having any enemies was going through her mind over and over.

She realized that she really didn't know all that much about Ben. At monthly staff meetings he didn't talk a lot about his past. He spent most of his time talking about the future and his plans and goals for the church.

His computer was on, but when she moved the mouse a screen with a login came up. She had no idea what his password might be. She began to look around at the other things in the room. She looked at the file cabinet briefly but soon dismissed it. She very much doubted that she'd find a file titled "Enemies". He had a desk calendar on the far edge of the desk and she walked over to look at it. The page for the day before had been torn out already.

She turned to leave the room when her eye caught a crumpled-up piece of paper far under the desk. She got down on the ground and stretched out her arm until she was able to reach it.

"What did you find?" Don asked as he walked in the room.

"I'm hoping it's a page from his day calendar," she said as she worked to smooth out the ball of paper. "It looks like it's the right size to be."

When she had the paper smoothed out she gasped. It was indeed the page from the day before and on it he had only one note.

J.S. 10 pm.

She started to feel dizzy and the room swam around her.

"What is it?" Don asked.

Silently she handed him the paper. He read it over then looked sharply at her.

"J.S.?"

She nodded.

"Jeremiah Silverman."

4

Cindy felt sick. Her dad crouched down next to her. "The police didn't find this," he said.

"Clearly not."

"Is there anyone else you know with the initials J.S.? Anyone who attends the church?"

Cindy wracked her brain, trying to think. "I know several Js but I can't think of any that have a last name that starts with S."

"We need to find out for sure."

"In the morning I can look it up in the church directory."

"You look pale. It's getting pretty late and we missed dinner. I suggest that we get something to eat, then get some sleep, and tackle this fresh in the morning," Don said.

She wanted to argue with him. She didn't want to do anything else until Jeremiah was cleared. She saw the wisdom in his suggestion, though. She couldn't help clear Jeremiah if she was so hungry and tired she couldn't think straight. She was still dizzy even after the initial shock of seeing his initials on the calendar page had passed.

"Who schedules an appointment for ten at night?" she asked.

"And on a Saturday no less. It's not like a pastor would need to be up early on Sunday," Don said drily.

Cindy tried to stand up and the room tilted around her.

"Whoa, you okay?" her dad asked, grabbing her elbow and steadying her.

She managed to get all the way to her feet. The room was still spinning, but not quite as badly.

"I think you're right. Food and sleep is the right choice. Just not the easy one," she said.

"I know. Call Harold and let's get out of here."

Cindy did and a minute later they were in the car heading back to Joseph's. They turned onto the street where the church and the synagogue were, and a sudden thought occurred to her. She needed to let Marie know what had happened. She didn't know her home number, but she remembered where she lived.

"I need to go let Jeremiah's secretary know what's happened, so she can handle things at the synagogue," Cindy said. "Turn right at the next light."

"So, she's the Jewish you?" her father asked, his tone light.

"I'm not sure she'd appreciate the comparison," Cindy said. "But she handles most of the daily business of the synagogue."

"So, the Jewish you."

"Yeah, but she doesn't have Geanie to help her."

"I really like Geanie. And Joseph."

"So do I. They have been great. They're always there for us."

"It's good to have friends like that in your life."

"Yes, it is. Turn right at the stop sign."

A couple of minutes later they arrived at Marie's house. Don parked at the curb.

"Do you want me to go in with you?" he asked.

"No, that's okay," she said.

She wasn't looking forward to this conversation and she kept imagining how Marie was going to react. Her feet felt like they were made of lead as she walked up to the front door. She rang the doorbell and waited, her misery mounting by the second.

Marie finally opened the door, a surprised look on her face. "Cindy, what are you doing here?"

"I need to let you know what's going on."

Marie glanced behind her and then stepped out onto the porch and closed the door behind her. "What's wrong?" she asked, lowering her voice.

"Two things. First, our head pastor, Ben, was murdered last night."

Marie's hand flew to her mouth, her eyes widening. "What? Who did it?"

"That's the second thing. They're accusing Jeremiah. The police arrested him."

Cindy expected anger, outrage, denial, fear, and disbelief from Marie. Instead the other woman became very still, her expression unreadable. After a moment Marie took a deep breath and folded her arms across her chest. She dropped her eyes.

"Did he do it?" Marie asked quietly.

Cindy stared at her in shock. "Of course not! How can you even ask me that?"

Marie looked up, her expression guarded. "I'm not an idiot. When he came to the synagogue, I was warned that he might need some looking after, some help integrating socially. I was given a number to call if he… if he couldn't… adapt. I didn't ask then. I've never asked. I don't want to know the details. I think it's better for everyone if I don't. But I have a pretty good idea what he's capable of, and I know that your pastor tried to get between you and Jeremiah."

"I don't know what to say."

Marie shook her head. "Don't say anything except for answering my question. It won't change what I do or how I act, but I need to know for my own sake."

"He didn't kill Ben," Cindy said. "And I'm going to find whoever did."

Marie nodded. "Good. If there's anything I can do to help, please let me know. I'll spin things at the synagogue as long as I can. Hopefully, he'll be cleared before anyone knows that he's more than just a witness."

Cindy reached out and hugged Marie. After a moment the other woman hugged her back. "I can't lose him," Cindy said, her voice breaking.

"I know," Marie said, stroking her back. "You won't. It will all work out. God has a plan and has brought you two together against all odds. He will not fail you now."

Cindy put her head down on Marie's shoulder as a sob escaped her. "You can do this," Marie whispered. "You are not alone. Make sure he knows that he isn't either."

"I will," Cindy said, straightening up.

Marie nodded.

"Thank you."

"You're welcome," Marie said, her voice unsteady. "Get some rest. Tomorrow's going to be a rough day for everyone."

"You, too."

Cindy turned and went back to the car. She dashed away her tears once she was inside.

"You okay?" her dad asked.

"Sometimes she surprises me," Cindy said.

"She'll handle things at the synagogue?"

"Yes, and she'll try to keep everything as much under wraps as she can."

"That's a blessing."

"She runs that place like a field general."

"That's good considering that come morning you'll all be under siege."

"I can't even think about work," Cindy said.

"Unfortunately, you're going to have to. Your coworkers are going to need you, and the parishioners are going to need all of you."

Cindy knew he was right, but she couldn't even imagine how she was going to be able to do anything until Jeremiah was freed.

"You and mom and Kyle should go home," she said.

"I'll see about sending them home, but I'm staying until this is done. You might need an outside perspective on some things."

"I can't ask you to go through this."

"You're not. I'm volunteering, and that's the end of the discussion."

~

Mark's anxiety and anger had given way to exhaustion. He was at his desk pouring over the files Keenan had compiled, looking for all the chinks in his case. To his relief he discovered that Keenan had no more on the terrorist at Joseph and Geanie's wedding than had been in Mark's report. That meant that of the one murder Jeremiah actually had committed there was nothing but purely circumstantial evidence. Keenan was using it, though, to try and show a pattern of Jeremiah killing to protect himself or his interests. He still hadn't put together that the terrorist had nothing to do with the crazy woman who had been trying to sabotage Joseph's wedding to another woman.

His notes on the homeless man who was murdered and died on Jeremiah's lawn were a bit more extensive as they included observations and suspicions that Not Paul had written down during the investigation. Although forensics had proven that the man was shot elsewhere and staggered quite a distance to where he died, Not Paul had still speculated that it was no accident that he had died on Jeremiah's lawn. He had concluded that the man knew Jeremiah in some way and that Jeremiah was lying about not knowing him.

That was true. Jeremiah had told Mark that he had known the man back when they were both spies overseas. That was, of course, something Jeremiah couldn't and wouldn't have admitted back when the body was found. Mark had also deduced from a later investigation that the man had been on his way to tell Jeremiah about what he'd witnessed in regard to the Iranian student's murder. All of that had tied into international terrorism and the events that had transpired in Jerusalem with Cindy and Jeremiah. Despite Not Paul's suspicions, there was nothing to hang Jeremiah with in that case either.

So far the only thing that he saw that connected Jeremiah to Ben was the fact that they knew each other, and that Ben had been vocally opposed to Jeremiah and Cindy getting married. The missing time in Joseph's surveillance system was suspicious, but not enough to convict Jeremiah with.

So, the real problem at the moment was Not Paul and the weapon that Keenan had found in Jeremiah's house. Jeremiah claimed it wasn't his and frankly, Mark believed him. The rabbi was right. He wouldn't have been stupid enough to keep that around.

"Detective Walters?"

Mark looked up and saw a man roughly his age wearing a suit that probably cost more than Mark made in a month. He was carrying a briefcase that also looked to be incredibly expensive.

"Yes?" Mark asked.

The man extended his hand. "My name is Bruce Westerfield of Price, Banner, and Westerfield law. I was told to speak with you."

"Oh, are you the attorney that Joseph called?" Mark asked, standing to shake the man's hand.

"The firm represents Mr. Coulter and he asked us to handle Rabbi Silverman's case."

"Well, you are most welcome here," Mark said fervently.

Usually he hated seeing a lawyer walk into the precinct because it almost always meant some dirtbag was not going to talk. It was a rare moment when he was glad to see one. Apparently it was rare enough in general that Bruce smiled at him.

"I wish I always received so warm a welcome from detectives."

"I can imagine."

"I'd like to see my client."

"Right this way," Mark said, quickly leading him back to the interrogation room where Jeremiah still was.

When Mark opened the door Keenan looked up, irritated.

"Jeremiah, your lawyer is here," Mark said, unable to keep the smugness from his voice. It did him good to see Keenan's scowl.

"Rabbi Silverman, my name is Bruce Westerfield, and I would like to offer my sincerest apologies for my delayed arrival."

"Hello," Jeremiah said, his voice neutral.

Bruce turned toward Detective Keenan. "Am I correct in assuming that you are Detective Keenan, the arresting officer?"

"You are," Keenan answered.

"Excellent, then I'll leave these with you," Bruce said, handing Keenan a stack of papers.

Keenan's scowl deepened. "What are these?"

"Direction from the Attorney General to release Rabbi Silverman from custody immediately and a complaint sworn out against you and the city police department for trespassing and fourth amendment violations."

"I had a warrant to search his home."

"His home, perhaps, but you were illegally present on Joseph Coulter's property when you forced your way into his home with neither a warrant nor probable cause."

Mark bit his lip to keep from laughing. The fourth amendment argument could be a sticky one, but given that Joseph had a fence around his property that Keenan and his officers had breached without permission or even notification, Keenan could be in trouble.

"And, just so you don't engage in illegal or harassing behavior in the future Judge Schofeld has issued restraining orders requiring you to keep a minimum distance of 100 yards away from Rabbi Silverman, Cindy Preston, Joseph Coulter, Geanie Coulter, and Traci Walters."

Mark had to hand it to Joseph's attorneys. They didn't mess around.

"A civil suit is also pending for defamation and use of excessive force."

"Excessive force? We barely touched him!"

"Seven police officers sent to arrest a rabbi. There is nothing about that which isn't excessive."

"You bastard."

"And one count of slander against myself regarding my parentage," Bruce said, completely unfazed.

"You might want to remember your Miranda rights," Mark said.

Keenan snarled at him and balled his hands into fists. "Mark, you will pay for this, I swear."

"Threatening a police officer and potentially assault. Shall we continue like this and see if we can add false arrest to your list of crimes?" Bruce asked Keenan.

"Get the hell out of here and take both of them with you!" Keenan roared.

Bruce nodded. "A pleasure doing business with you. Gentlemen, let's go."

Bruce turned and strode out the door. Jeremiah got up and followed him and Mark turned to trail after.

Once in the parking lot Bruce shook both their hands. "Gentlemen, I will speak with you both tomorrow."

"Thank you," Jeremiah said.

"No, Rabbi Silverman, thank you for all your service to your community," Bruce said.

"You're good," Mark told him with a grin.

Bruce's lips twitched. "Mr. Coulter doesn't pay us to be good. He pays us to be the best."

"Well, he's certainly getting his money's worth."

"Thank you," Bruce said. "Good evening."

He got in his car and headed out.

"Let's get out of here," Mark said steering Jeremiah toward his car.

"I couldn't agree more."

As soon as they had driven out of the parking lot Mark heaved a sigh of relief. "Wow, I'm glad Bruce is on our side."

"Me, too," Jeremiah said, his voice tense.

"We're going to get out of this," Mark reassured him.

"I'm glad you're confident," Jeremiah said.

"Isn't this the kind of mess your old employer should sweep under the rug?" Mark asked.

"If my old employer were my *current* employer then yes, that could absolutely happen. However, given the fact that it is previous and not current there's no help coming from that quarter."

"Unless you give your old employer a reason to help," Mark said.

Jeremiah cocked his head to the side. "Like what?"

"Rejoin the fold."

Jeremiah shook his head. "Not going to happen."

"Okay, then how about handing them an international terror ring?"

Jeremiah nodded slowly. "They might be inclined to help if the stakes were that high."

"That's what I'm thinking."

"So, what's your plan?"

"You just heard it," Mark said.

"That's it?" Jeremiah asked.

"Yup."

"You realize as plans go that's pretty simplistic, right?" Jeremiah asked.

"It's a work in progress. We know two of four murders were terror related."

"You mean Peter and the actual terrorist?"

"Yes, those two."

"Okay," Jeremiah said, the doubt evident in his voice.

"I know I'm grasping at straws, but we could be in real trouble here," Mark said. "We've built this whole house of cards over the last few years and it's in serious danger of all coming down right on top of us."

"I won't let this come down on you," Jeremiah said.

Mark rolled his eyes. "I don't know how you think you could stop that. You go down for murder and I'll be lucky if all they think is that I'm incompetent and unfit for the job."

Jeremiah didn't say anything.

"Look, tell me what you're thinking. I've spent too much time in my own head the last few hours."

"You don't want to know what I'm thinking," Jeremiah said quietly.

Mark glanced at him. "If you're thinking about killing Keenan, then you're right, I don't want to know, because that will just make things worse at this point. Look, there's only one good way out of this, and that's for everyone to realize you're innocent. Then we can all go back to our normal lives."

Jeremiah chuckled.

"What?"

"You said 'normal lives'. What we have are nothing like normal lives."

"Okay, then normal for us. I'd settle for that."

"So, you want to go hunting terrorists and find a way to pin this all on them?"

"Yes," Mark said. "I think that's a solid play."

"You realize if you pull in the organizations that deal with terrorists that all of this could go completely sideways, right?"

"Is that your way of saying that the Mossad and the C.I.A. are unpredictable?"

"Far from it. They are sometimes a little too predictable, especially when it comes to downsides."

"I'm not seeing where we have a whole lot of other options," Mark said.

"We need to give this some serious thought," Jeremiah said. "We can't make a snap decision on this."

"Well, two more minutes and we'll be back at Joseph and Geanie's and then we can all sleep on it."

They made it past the fence and then climbed the hill to the house. Once there they parked. Mark was about to turn off the car when Jeremiah grabbed his arm.

"What?" he asked.

"On the ground, do you see that?" Jeremiah asked, voice tense.

"It looks like someone painted something on the ground," Mark said with a frown. "I don't remember anything being there the last few days."

"Turn on your high beams so we can get a better look at it," Jeremiah said.

Mark did and then they both got out of the car. Once they did the smell of stale blood hit Mark's nostrils and the hair on the back of his neck stood on end.

"The writing is in blood," Jeremiah said, confirming his fears.

Mark looked down and could see the whole thing. Once he read it he looked at Jeremiah as panic welled up in him. "What does that mean?"

On the ground in blood was spelled out *malakh ha-mavet.*

Jeremiah clenched his fists. "It means we don't have to go looking for terrorists. They've found us."

5

Cindy, Geanie, and Traci were sitting around the kitchen counter, holding hands and praying. At the moment it was all that they could do.

Her mother and brother were upstairs asleep. Her father's attempts to persuade them to leave had failed. She was sorry for that because dealing with them was not what she needed. She even got the feeling that Kyle was relieved that Jeremiah had been arrested and was in serious trouble. For that alone she wished she could be throwing darts at his picture like she used to.

The twins were upstairs asleep and a baby monitor on the counter enabled Traci to hear if they woke up. Joseph had come home from the emergency church meeting just a couple minutes before and had gone upstairs to shower.

That left the three of them to sit and watch and pray. Traci's husband was with Jeremiah at the precinct and she'd already said there was no way she was sleeping until he came back. Geanie was refusing to sleep until Cindy did.

Cindy couldn't sleep, not yet. Maybe after they heard from Mark she'd try to, but she didn't believe she would be able to fall asleep with all the worry and fear that were filling her. She was sick to her stomach and she was jumping at every noise. Every time Blackie or one of the dogs had come into the room she'd jumped. They'd finally put them all to bed.

They kept taking turns praying. Geanie prayed with a ringing voice, filled with passion and conviction. Traci prayed softly, hesitantly, unused to praying as she was. Her words were heartfelt, though, and brought Cindy to the brink of tears more than once. Cindy herself was all over the map, praying a torrent of words one minute and then barely able to put together two words the next.

She was struggling to find the words she wanted when she heard what sounded like someone running behind her. She turned around as Jeremiah raced into the room.

She screamed and jumped to her feet, throwing her arms around his neck a second later. She hugged him and kissed him, crying all the while. He hugged her back fiercely for a moment and then she recognized that he was asking her something, but she was too overwhelmed to make sense of his words.

"Joseph's upstairs showering," Geanie said.

"The kids are also upstairs, asleep," Traci said.

"What?" Cindy asked as Jeremiah pulled away from her.

"Your family, your parents, Kyle, where are they?"

"Upstairs. They went to bed a while ago. Why?" she asked.

"We've got trouble," Mark said as he came into the room.

Traci jumped up and went to kiss Mark.

"Trouble? What kind of trouble?" Cindy asked. "The police let you go, right?"

"For now, thanks to Joseph's lawyer," Mark said. "He's still in hot water. It's worse than that, though."

"What could possibly be worse?" Geanie asked the question before Cindy could.

"My enemies have found me. They wrote the words *malakh ha-mavet* in blood just outside the front door," Jeremiah said.

"No," Cindy whispered, feeling suddenly faint.

"What's going on?" she heard Joseph ask right before he appeared in the doorway. He saw Jeremiah and grinned. "Excellent! I knew they couldn't hold you for long. I hope Bruce was helpful."

"Extremely," Mark said. "But we're not out of the woods yet."

"What does *malakh ha-mavet* mean?" Traci asked.

"Angel of Death. It's what they used to call Jeremiah," Cindy said.

"Wait, where was this?" Joseph asked.

"Just outside by the cars," Jeremiah said.

Joseph turned and headed for the entry.

"Don't go out there!" Jeremiah commanded, his voice booming.

Joseph froze in mid-step then turned slowly around. "Are we in trouble?" he asked.

"Yes," Jeremiah said. "We all are."

"The timing can't be a coincidence," Traci said.

"I was thinking the same thing," Joseph said. "Is it possible that whoever wrote that killed Ben and framed you?"

"With these people anything is possible," Jeremiah said.

That was the truth. Cindy knew that firsthand. The last time they'd been confronted with Jeremiah's past it had brought them together, but she was terrified that this time it would tear them apart.

Over the baby monitor they could hear one of the children start to cry. Traci got up and hurried off. They were all silent for a minute until they heard her speaking softly to Ryan.

"We have to get them out of here," Cindy said.

"We all have to get out of here," Jeremiah said.

"Alright, where do we go that's safe?" Joseph asked.

It was a valid question, but no one seemed to have an answer.

"Look, we're all tired. I suggest we lock the house down tight, get a few hours of sleep and figure this out in the morning," Mark said.

"But what if whoever wrote that is waiting for us to do just that?" Geanie asked.

"They won't strike tonight. They'll wait and strike when they can cause the most panic," Jeremiah said.

"So, it's settled. Sleep now, plan later," Mark said.

Cindy wasn't sure that was the best idea, but Jeremiah wasn't objecting so neither did she.

"Cindy, I'll walk you to your room," Jeremiah said.

The others trailed out of the kitchen with them, all heading for the stairs. They climbed in silence and each step felt like a dozen as she dragged her tired body upward.

When they made it to her room, Jeremiah walked in and checked it out before giving her the all-clear to come in. Once she did he wrapped his arms around her and kissed her.

"I'm so sorry," he whispered moments later.

"This isn't your fault," she hastened to reassure him.

"I can't lose you," he said.

"I can't lose you, either."

When he finally made to leave panic surged through her and she clung to his arm.

"What is it?" he asked, turning back to her.

"I'm worried something is going to happen to you," she said.

He took a deep breath. "I know, but I'll do everything I can to keep us safe."

He finally pulled free and left the room, closing the door behind him.

~

Leaving the room was one of the hardest things Jeremiah had ever done. He wanted to stay with Cindy, to wrap her in his arms and keep her safe. He knew, though, without a shadow of a doubt that he couldn't protect her that way. Sooner or later someone would come for them and he'd be too distracted to notice until it was too late.

He couldn't let that happen. If ever those he loved needed his strength it was now. He could do what needed to be done, no matter what it cost. He could because the alternative was too terrible.

He knew the way these people thought. They were masters at inflicting terror. The message had been designed to do just that. It was meant to send him and those around him into a blind panic. He couldn't allow that to happen. He needed to be clear-headed and rational no matter what it took.

Very shortly they'd target one of the people in the house and kill them. They'd likely start with either Geanie or Traci. They'd torture and kill whichever lady they chose in such a way as to create maximum fear and chaos. Then they'd do it again and again. They'd save Cindy for the last. They'd make him watch as they killed her.

Trying to run and hide at this point wasn't a viable option. They knew who his friends were, and they'd be watching. No matter how careful they were, they wouldn't be able to stop those who were coming after them. He had only one real choice if there was to be even a prayer of them all surviving. He picked up his phone and dialed a number he had memorized.

"Rabbi? It's late," Martin said, yawning.

He had clearly woken the C.I.A. agent. He hoped that meant that he was in the country. It was already daytime overseas. His last contact with Martin had been just a few days earlier and it had been in town. If he was very lucky the man was still local.

"Are you nearby?"

"Why?"

"I need help and there's no one else I trust."

"I don't like hearing that."

"I don't like saying it," Jeremiah told him.

"I'm listening," Martin said, sounding suddenly awake.

"You know that problem you warned me about?"

"Yes."

"It's here."

"I was afraid you were going to say that. Tell me what you need."

~

Mark stared at the big, comfy bed in his and Traci's room at the mansion and yawned. "I'm going to sleep hard tonight," he said.

"I hope we all do," Traci said fervently. "Tomorrow's going to be busy."

Mark snorted. "That's putting it mildly."

"I can't even begin to imagine what Cindy's going through," Traci said with a shudder. "She, Geanie, and I spent some time praying tonight."

"Yeah?" Mark asked, not as surprised as he once would have been.

Traci nodded. "At least it felt like I was doing something, helping."

"Jeremiah needs all the help he can get."

"You don't think he's going to do something stupid do you?"

Mark sighed and sat down on the edge of the bed. "Define stupid."

"You know what I mean."

"I wish I could say "no" but he can be pretty bull-headed sometimes."

"Reminds me of someone else I know," Traci teased as she moved close and began to massage his shoulders, careful not to injure the one that was still recovering from the knife wound.

"Please, I'm positively docile and compliant by comparison."

Traci laughed, and the sound warmed him through and through.

"Have I told you today how amazing you are?" he asked.

"Not that I remember."

"Well, shame on me."

Before either of them could say anything else there was a knock on the door. Mark got up with a groan. "It better not be another crisis. I can't handle any more for the day."

"Technically it's already tomorrow."

"Not until I sleep it's not."

"If we went by that we'd be a couple of years behind the rest of the world."

"Frightening, but probably accurate," he said.

He opened the door and saw Jeremiah standing there. The man's face was a blank mask. Mark hated when he did that.

"I need to see you guys downstairs in ten minutes."

"Can it wait until morning?" Mark asked even though he was pretty sure he knew the answer.

"It really can't."

"Okay."

Mark closed the door and turned to Traci. "I have a feeling we're about to lose another day in our calendar."

~

When Cindy got downstairs to the living room she found that Joseph, Geanie, Mark, Traci, and her father were already there. She took a seat on the couch and looked around. "I guess I'm late to the party."

"I think we were early," Traci said. "Jeremiah gave us ten minutes to get down here."

"He gave us five and that was five minutes ago," Joseph said with a frown.

"Me, too," Don said.

"He just told me "now" and hurried off," Cindy said.

"Why stagger it?" Traci asked.

"So that we didn't have time to all confer together?" Mark guessed.

"But why?" Cindy asked. "That makes no-"

She stopped as she heard the front door open and close. Moments later Jeremiah walked into the room.

"I'm glad you're all here," he said, his face a mask.

"Jeremiah, what's going on?" she asked as an icy knot of dread settled into her stomach.

~

Jeremiah didn't answer Cindy directly. He was finding it difficult just to look at her. What he was about to do was hard enough as it was, and he couldn't lose his resolve. Not now.

"My enemies are coming at me from all sides," Jeremiah said. "This is my fault. I've gotten careless. I can't involve the rest of you any more than I already have."

They all stared at him. Some looked puzzled, others afraid. Mark looked angry.

"You care to explain what you mean by that?" Mark demanded.

Jeremiah looked his friend in the eyes. He knew he had one chance to do this right and he had to appeal to the detective on a personal level, in a way that he would understand and hopefully respect.

"Brother, I can't risk losing you. You mean too much to me and it would destroy me if something happened to you, my sister, my niece or my nephew."

Tears sprang to Mark's eyes and he dropped his head down as a shudder passed through him. Traci grabbed his hand and Mark clung to it like a drowning man.

Jeremiah turned to Joseph and Geanie. "My friends, it was never my intention to bring danger to your home. The two of you have sheltered us all many times. You have offered love and protection. It's time to return that favor."

Joseph and Geanie exchanged puzzled looks.

Jeremiah turned to Cindy. "My love, my life. I would die for you. I would die without you. My heart is yours in this world and what will come after. Never doubt that."

She looked like she was about to say something, but he turned swiftly to Don. "Please, take care of her."

Don nodded but didn't say anything.

"You're not doing this by yourself," Traci said, the first one to speak up. "And if you think we're going to just sit by and let you, you're crazy. We're helping, and you can't stop us."

The moment of truth had arrived. Pain surged through him and he did everything he could to push it out of his mind. He couldn't let his emotions cloud his judgment or he might as well lie down and die. He looked at each face, marking them in his memory. They had each become important to him, even Don, who had offered to be the father that Jeremiah had lost.

"Where I'm going none of you can follow. I know you'll try and I can't risk any of you getting hurt. I'm sorry, but this is the way it has to be."

He turned toward the foyer, and Martin and four other men dressed in tactical gear entered the room. Martin nodded at him and Jeremiah nodded back. Then he turned for one last look at all the people in the world that he held dear.

"Goodbye," he said, before turning and making his way quickly to the front door. He opened it, and stepped out into the night.

6

Cindy lunged up from her seat with a cry as Jeremiah left. She started to follow, but her dad stood up, grabbed her, and pulled her into a tight embrace. She struggled to break free, but he just held her tighter.

"You have to let him go," he whispered.

"No! He needs me, and I need him. We're stronger together."

"Cindy, it had to be this way," Martin said.

She twisted around so she could glare at him. "You of all people should know that I can help him. I've done it before. I'm not going to just sit and wait to hear that he's been killed!"

"He has work to do that you can't be a part of," Martin said. "Any of you," he added, looking around the room.

"And just who are you?" Mark demanded.

"You can call me Martin. I'm a colleague of Jeremiah's."

"You're the C.I.A. agent from Vegas," Mark said.

"He is," Cindy said, still glaring.

"Now that introductions are out of the way, it's time to move all of you to a secure location," Martin said.

"I'm not going," Cindy said.

Martin grimaced. "Jeremiah says that you are, no matter what I have to do to make that happen."

"It's best we go with them now," her dad spoke up.

Cindy wanted to argue, to scream and cry and rage, but the fight was leaving her and in its place grief and fear were taking hold. She stopped trying to break free from her dad and instead began to lean against him, no longer certain her legs would fully support her.

"If someone would like to go upstairs and get the other four members of our party, that would be great," Martin said.

Mark and Traci stepped forward. Martin signaled and one of his men escorted them out of the room. They returned less than five minutes later with both babies, Kyle, and Cindy's mom in tow.

Carol and Kyle were blustering. Cindy leaned her head into her dad's shoulder, unable to cope with either of them.

"Both of you knock it off," Don barked.

Cindy glanced up just in time to see the startled looks on her mother and brother's faces. She couldn't honestly remember her father using that tone of voice before. It was evidence of just how seriously he was taking the events that were unfolding around them.

"Dad-" Kyle began.

"I don't want to hear it," Don said. "Lives are on the line, including ours. Not a peep from either of you until we get where we're going. Understood?"

Both her mom and Kyle nodded without saying anything.

"Alright, we're moving out," Martin said.

~

Jeremiah watched from a perch on the roof of the house while Martin and his team loaded Cindy and the others into black sedans. He didn't know where they were being taken, at his own request. He did know that they would be safe no matter what. He waited, watching them and the surrounding area.

Mark and Traci were each holding one of the twins, one of whom was fussing slightly. Kyle and Carol both looked furious, but Don seemed to have them under control. Everyone in the house had to go into hiding, hard as that would be.

Slowly the cars moved out, and moments later they were heading down the hill. As soon as they were off Joseph and Geanie's property, Jeremiah breathed a sigh of relief.

He could do what he had to now that he didn't have to worry about anyone else. The night pressed in around him and he started to remember what it was like to live with the silence and to pick out the slightest changes in his environment. It was years since he had been truly alone, but the old skills were still there. They always had been.

He was ready. He had some cash on him for things he might need that he had taken from a safe Joseph kept in his office. He'd pay the man back if he could one day. Cindy and the others were safe, and it was time for him to go to work.

~

They had all been split up into four cars. That alone would have been enough to set Mark on edge. What made it worse was the way they'd been split up. Each car had two agents in the front, one driving and one literally riding shotgun. That left room for three in each back seat. He had heard enough from Martin to know that all four cars were taking a different route to wherever it was that they were going. That made the separation anxiety he was experiencing even more intense.

Mark, Traci, and Ryan were in the back of one car. Traci was wedged in the middle between Mark and Ryan's car seat. They had been separated from Rachel. At least Rachel was with Joseph and Geanie and that gave him some comfort. Don was with Carol and Kyle. Mark didn't envy Don the conversation that must be happening in that car.

That left Cindy all alone with Martin and another agent. That really worried him more than he could say. His own natural paranoia developed over years of being a cop and years knowing her and Jeremiah was kicking into high gear. How did they really know they could trust Martin? How did they know that was even his real name?

For all they knew he was the enemy and he had specifically chosen a name that would subconsciously set Cindy at ease because it started with the same three letters that Mark's name did. That way it would sound familiar, like someone that could be trusted, like a friend.

He couldn't see anything outside the tinted windows and his anxiety skyrocketed. This could be the most insidious kidnapping plot ever.

He forced himself to try and take deep breaths. Jeremiah apparently trusted this guy otherwise he wouldn't have sent them all off with him. Even if he did trust Martin, though, he'd been wrong to do what he did.

Mark was furious at Jeremiah and at himself. He should have known the rabbi would pull some kind of lone wolf crap given the circumstances and how he'd been acting right before siccing the C.I.A. on them. He shouldn't be trying to go it alone, shutting out his friends in the process. They all worked well as a team and he was benching them all. He was mad at himself for deep down being grateful that Jeremiah had taken the rest of them out of play.

He wanted Traci and the twins to be safe. That was the most important thing to him. Jeremiah's plan for that seemed a bit extreme, but he knew the types of people he was going up against and they didn't. Mark did trust that Jeremiah had done what he had thinking it was in everyone's best interest. Mark just wished that he had been consulted.

"What are you thinking?" Traci asked him quietly.

"I'm really mad at him."

"I know. I can tell," she said.

"He had no right to do this."

"He probably felt like he did. That it was his duty to keep us all safe."

"Dear heavens, you sound like him," Mark said.

"I'll take that as a compliment," she said.

"By going off the reservation he's not only screwed himself but also the rest of us. He's a suspect in four murder cases and it will not go unnoticed that he's gone off the grid."

"Mark, just say what it is you're afraid to say," Traci said quietly.

Mark swallowed hard. "I don't want to," he whispered. "I don't want this to all be real."

Traci grabbed his hand and squeezed it hard. He could feel tears welling in his eyes. He was exhausted, and it had been an emotionally charged day. He needed to sleep soon before he was no good to anyone, but he was terrified of what would happen if he did fall asleep. There was a very real possibility that when he woke his world would have changed forever.

"Say it," Traci urged.

"I'm afraid that I'll never see Jeremiah again."

"Why?"

"Because in the next few days he's either going to be killed or he's going to have to go on the run for the rest of his life. His only chance will be to flee this country and change his identity or else risk being caught and going to jail for murder. Keenan won't give up, and once he finds out Jeremiah is gone, there's going to be a manhunt on for him."

"And?"

Mark took a shaky breath. "And if they think I helped him, the same could be true for me."

Traci leaned over, hugging him as best as she could. "We'll get through this, like we've made it through everything else life has thrown at us," she whispered.

"What if we can't this time?" he asked, nearly choking on his own fear.

"Then we'll run together," Traci said.

Tears slid down his cheeks. "I can't do that to you, to Ryan and Rachel."

"Well, you for sure can't do it without us. Whatever happens, I'm with you to the end, do you understand?"

"Yes," Mark said.

As the car sped on into the night they clung to each other and cried.

~

Cindy glared at Martin who was sitting beside her in the back of the car. She was the only one in the group who had been completely isolated from the rest. The first thing she'd done once they'd started driving was tried the door, but it was locked with no way for her to unlock it.

"Nice to see you, too," he said wryly.

"What idiotic plan have the two of you hatched without me this time?"

Martin pushed a button and raised the privacy glass between the front and back seats.

"No plan. I just agreed to protect all of you while he handles what he needs to handle."

"He needs me."

"Yes, he needs you safe."

"He needs me to be out there helping him. Even if he manages to find and kill whoever is out to get him the charges against him aren't just going to go away. I need to figure out who killed Pastor Ben and why."

Martin sighed. "I'll be honest with you, Cindy. Jeremiah has more lives than a cat, but I don't see a way out of this for him."

"There's always a way out," she snapped.

"Given what all of you have gone through I'm sure it's begun to seem that way. Some things can't be fixed, though, and sometimes we can't escape the consequences of our actions no matter how well-intentioned we are or how unfair it would be."

"What are you saying?"

"I'm saying, some problems are permanent. Sometimes people die no matter what we do to save them."

The sick feeling in her stomach that she'd had earlier came back in full force. "You think he's going to die, don't you?"

Martin sighed and turned away from her. "I think we've done everything we can to give him a fighting chance. And he'd be the first to tell you that if he lives but the people he cares about are killed, it wouldn't be worth it. I owe him. And I'm doing the best I can by limiting the number of things he needs to worry about."

"If I remember correctly I was the one who figured out that the Dome of the Chain was the real target back in Israel. So, by my calculations you owe me, too."

"That's true."

"So, let me go help him."

"I can't do that."

"Why not?" she demanded, her frustration raging out of control.

"Because I have a family that I need to be able to go home to."

"What does that have to do with anything?"

"If I keep you locked up for your own safety you'll only hate me for it. If I let you go, Jeremiah will kill me."

"No, he wouldn't," she said.

"Then you really don't know him as well as you think you do," he said.

More than anything else he could have said, that statement unsettled her. "I do know him, he wouldn't do that."

"Just because you bring a tiger into your house and teach it to play nice with you and your family doesn't make it any less of a predator. Jeremiah is a killer and that's something that doesn't just go away. There's a reason he was so good at his job, a reason he became famous in the community."

"His faith. He believed absolutely in the rightness of what he was doing," Cindy said.

Martin shook his head. "I don't doubt his devotion, but that's just what helped him sleep at night, it's not what made him great."

"What made him great?"

"You can only train a man to do so much, go so far. For them to cross over and be able to do the kinds of things Jeremiah did it has to be in their blood. The Mossad didn't turn him into a killer, they just gave him a target."

"I think that is an incredibly pessimistic point of view," Cindy said, struggling with a way to refute what he'd just said.

"You can think what you want, but I am on your side. I'm not like Jeremiah, although I have known one or two others like him."

Cindy took a deep breath and lifted her chin in defiance. "You can think what you want, but I know the truth. And you should know that I will find a way to escape and I will go and help him."

"Yeah, good luck with that."

"You don't think I can escape?" she asked.

"No, you're clever and resourceful. If you put your mind to it you could probably find a way."

"Then what?" she asked.

"Even if you do escape, you'll never find him."

"Of course, I will."

Martin laughed out loud. "Cindy, Jeremiah's off the grid. He ditched his phone back at the house. He's gone completely dark which means I couldn't even find him if I tried."

"What are you saying?" she asked.

"I'm saying he's gone and none of us can help him now."

7

It felt like they had been driving forever when they finally stopped. Mark had lost track of the number of turns at some point, so he had absolutely no idea where they were. They could be in downtown Pine Springs or forty miles away for all he knew.

The wound in his shoulder ached. He had rebandaged it. Fortunately, it had only been a small tear in the skin that had been bleeding back at the precinct. Still, it was far from healed. Between him, Cindy, and Liam they were the walking wounded.

Liam. He had no idea what his partner was going to think or what Martin was going to tell him or the captain about Mark's absence. There was nothing he could do about it at the moment so it was going to have to be tomorrow's problem.

The car remained stopped. His door opened, and he saw that they were in an underground parking area. He motioned for Traci to stay put before he slowly got out of the car and looked around.

The two agents from their car were standing there, faces inscrutable.

"Where are the others?" Mark asked, noticing that theirs was the only car there.

"We are the first to arrive," the driver said. "As per the plan."

"Oh yeah? What's next in the plan?" Mark asked.

"We wait."

Mark was getting more and more agitated. All of this felt so wrong to him. Unfortunately, his gun was still back at the mansion, in the dresser drawer in his and Traci's room where he had left it when he thought he was about to turn in for the night.

He took a deep breath. Even if he did have it this would be no time to engage in hostilities with these men. Traci and Ryan were in the car and he couldn't risk them getting hurt.

"I want my daughter," Mark growled.

"She'll be here shortly," the driver said.

Mark looked around, but could see no distinguishing markings. If they were in a public parking garage there would be signs for rows and exits, but he didn't see any such thing.

"Where are we?" he asked.

"Underground."

"Well, duh," he said, letting the sarcasm drip from his words.

"That is all I'm authorized to tell you."

"Great," Mark muttered. "Well, if we're waiting, I'm going to wait back in the car.

He got into the backseat again and closed the door.

"What's going on?" Traci asked, her voice fearful.

"We're the first ones here. Apparently, it was planned that way. We're in an underground structure, but I have a feeling it's private or government owned from the looks of it.

"What do we do?"

"Wait. That's all we can do right now," he said.

Ryan whimpered, and Mark thought he was waking up. A moment later, though, his son settled back down.

"It's just a bad dream," Traci reassured him.

"I wish I could say the same," Mark said.

"We need to update our wills," Traci said suddenly.

Mark felt his heart stutter. He grabbed her hand. "Honey, we're going to be okay," he said, although he knew it could be a lie.

"If something happens to us I want Joseph and Geanie to raise Ryan and Rachel," Traci said.

Mark nodded. "I can live with that."

More like I could die with that, he thought to himself, since if that happened he wouldn't be around to see it.

"I think someone else is coming," Traci said suddenly.

He listened, and he heard the hum of an engine. He knocked on the window and the driver opened his door again. Mark started to get out of the car, but then hastily rethought that when he saw that the other agent had brought his shotgun up to his shoulder and was training it on the black sedan driving slowly toward them.

"Should we be concerned?" Mark asked.

"No, we have this," the driver said, pulling a gun from his shoulder holster.

Mark froze, half-in, half-out of the car as the sedan rolled to a gentle stop. It flashed its headlights four times then turned off the engine. The front doors opened, and two agents stepped carefully out of the vehicle. Mark recognized the one who had been inside the mansion when Jeremiah left.

"Bravo, one, one, three. Packages are secure. No footprints," the driver said.

The agent with the shotgun immediately lowered it and Mark's driver reholstered his gun. The agents from the other car opened the back doors and Geanie and Joseph stepped out quickly.

"It's Geanie and Joseph," Mark told Traci.

"Rachel is with them, right?" she asked, her voice tight.

Geanie leaned back into the car and a few seconds later pulled Rachel out.

"Yes," Mark said, relief flooding him.

Traci climbed out of the car and pushed past him as she rushed toward Geanie and Rachel. A moment later she was hugging both of them. Geanie was crying as she hugged Traci back.

"This is insane," Mark muttered to himself.

He could swear he saw the driver smirk slightly.

He climbed back into the car and freed Ryan from his car seat. The baby yawned but kept his eyes tight shut.

"Wish I could do that," Mark said.

He walked over to the others and reassured himself that Rachel was okay as he looked down at her sleeping form. Geanie was clinging to her as fiercely as if she were her own child. He realized that she and Joseph would make fantastic parents some day and that any child would be lucky to have them.

A distant rumble caught his attention and he turned to see that all four agents were now training weapons on a car approaching from the far side of the complex. Mark felt his mouth go dry as he wondered if the car held friend or foe.

It stopped several yards away and flashed its lights twice before turning them off. He remembered the other car had flashed its lights four times.

"Is that good?" he asked anxiously.

"So far so good," the driver of his car said.

The doors opened, and the two agents got out of the third car. "Charlie, one, one, three," the driver announced.

Everyone lowered their weapons.

"This is getting nerve wracking," Mark confided in the others.

Agents opened the back doors and Don, Carol, and Kyle exited.

Mark winced slightly. He'd been hoping to see Cindy come out of the car. Instead he was stuck with her obnoxious brother and clueless Mom. Don exited like a man who had experience being in similar situations. He looked around and then focused his eyes on Mark.

"Where's Cindy?" he asked.

"I don't know. Apparently, they've staggered our arrivals on purpose."

Don didn't look any more pleased by that than Mark was.

"This is an outrage," Carol said.

"Mom, be quiet," Kyle said as he took in the men with guns.

Mark gave him points for that. At least he was learning when he needed to button up and let others do the talking.

Carol looked outraged, but did as her son said.

"Where are we?" Joseph asked.

"Underground," Mark said, offering up the only piece of information he had. It wasn't much, but sometimes even a tiny shard of information could help.

They all fell silent, standing, waiting. It reminded him of a play Traci had dragged him to years and years before when they were still dating. He leaned toward her, "What was that play-"

"Waiting for Godot," she said before he could finish asking her the question.

"That's the one," he said.

Another couple of minutes passed as they waited. Finally, a fourth car came into sight.

Guns up, Mark thought. *Almost comical at this point.*

The sedan rolled to a stop, flashed its lights three times, and turned off its engine. Two agents got out of the car. "Alpha, one, one, three," the driver called out.

Everyone lowered their guns and Mark held his breath as the agents opened the back doors of the latest arrival.

Cindy and Martin stepped out and everyone surged forward to greet her.

"Everyone with me," Martin said, turning and leading the way to one of the walls.

The agents managed to surround them so that they had no choice but to move forward. They reached a door and Martin pressed his hand against a plate on the wall next to it. The door opened and they all began moving down a long corridor behind it.

The farther away from the cars they walked the more trapped Mark felt. Apparently he wasn't the only one.

"Does anyone have a cell?" Joseph murmured under his breath.

Cindy and Mark shook their heads.

"What did he say?" Carol asked loudly.

Cindy visibly cringed.

"He wanted to know if any of you had a cell," Martin said without turning around. "The answer is 'no'. We can't risk you contacting the outside world and exposing yourselves to danger."

"We can't just disappear off the face of the earth," Mark protested. "We have jobs, people that will notice if we're suddenly missing."

"Geanie and I are supposed to be at church in the morning to help handle things in the wake of the pastor's murder," Cindy said.

"Your absences will be handled," Martin said confidently. "It's not like we've never done something like this before."

"That doesn't make me feel any better," Geanie murmured.

"What about our pets? You hustled us out of the mansion before we could get them. We'll need to call a sitter," Joseph said worriedly. "We'll need a phone to do that."

"No need to worry about them. We got them all out first," Martin said.

"You did?" Joseph asked.

Martin opened the door and in the room beyond they saw Captain, Buster, Clarice, and Blackie. Traci ran forward and threw her arms around Buster who went crazy licking her face.

"Always save the cat, or the dog, as the case may be," Martin said with a smile.

"It makes your prisoners more compliant," Cindy said bitterly.

"Not prisoners. Recalcitrant guests," Martin said, his expression unwavering. "After you."

They all filed into the room. Martin and one of the agents came with them and the rest stayed in the corridor. Martin closed the door and Mark felt even more trapped as they were sealed into the room.

It was a large space, comfortable looking with chairs scattered around a living area in the center. There were beds around the perimeter of the room, including two cribs, and what looked like a couple of small bathrooms. There was a refrigerator, a sink, and a microwave. On a dining table were stacks of books and games.

On the wall next to the door that they had come through was another hand scanner. They were going to be locked in. Above it was what looked like an intercom.

"This is kidnapping," Mark said quietly.

"Protective custody. As a cop you should be familiar with that concept," Martin said, smiling at him.

Mark wanted to punch the man right in the face. He was still holding Ryan, though, so there was nothing he could do at the moment.

"Hopefully this won't be necessary for very long," Martin said. "Frankly, I don't anticipate it will be. I suggest you view this as a safe place and enjoy a little vacation from the outside world. There are activities and food available to you. I or another agent will check on you at least once a day to see how you are, restock the food, etc. Any questions?"

"What if there's an emergency?" Geanie asked.

Martin pointed to the intercom above the hand scanner. "You can use this at any time to speak with agents on guard duty. If there is a *legitimate* emergency they will help." He stared directly at Cindy as he emphasized the word "legitimate". She folded her arms across her chest and gave him a defiant look.

"How will we walk the dogs?" Joseph asked.

Martin pointed to a far corner of the room. "Litter box for the cat and those fake lawn things for the dogs. There's deodorizer and the air filtration system is top notch. And before you ask, there's a diaper disposal machine over by the baby stuff," he said, pointing to another section of the room.

Mark had to hand it to him, the man was prepared.

"Right now, I suggest you all try and get some sleep," Martin said.

He turned, placed his hand on the scanner, and Mark could hear the door unlock. Both agents went out the door and closed it and they were sealed in again.

There was a second of silence and then pandemonium broke out. Ryan began to cry as Cindy slammed her fist down on the dining room table.

"What is going on here?" Carol shouted as Kyle ran to the door and tried to open it. He continued yanking on the door until he was red in the face.

Hearing her brother woke up Rachel and soon she was crying as well. The dogs began to bark in agitation and the noise became deafening.

Joseph sat down heavily on one of the chairs at the table and put his head in his hands as Geanie tried to shush Rachel. Mark stood, bouncing Ryan gently up and down, but his son just cried harder and harder.

Carol was still shouting, and no one was answering her. Kyle had switched to beating the door with his fists, a lot of good that would do. Traci was vainly trying to calm down the dogs.

"Quiet!" Don roared unexpectedly.

Everyone stopped talking and when they did the dogs stopped barking. Even Rachel and Ryan quieted down as though heeding the older man's command.

"Now is not the time to fall apart," Don said. "We've got to think through this clearly and rationally. We're safe for the moment and we're all together. That's important."

Cindy turned to him. "No, we're not all together. Jeremiah is out there somewhere, risking his life right now."

"I know, honey, but there's nothing we can do about that," Don said.

"That's where you're wrong. There is something we can do about it."

"What?" Mark asked.

Cindy looked at him and there was fire blazing in her eyes. "We're going to escape."

8

"How?" Kyle asked.

Cindy turned to look at her brother. "We fake an emergency, and when someone comes in we hit them over the head with something, like that lamp," she said pointing to one on a stand between two of the beds.

"Great," Kyle said, starting toward the lamp.

"Not great," Mark said.

"Why?" Cindy asked.

"Because your plan only takes care of one guard and gets us out of this room. There are probably other guards and security measures between us and the outside world," Don said. "Getting into and out of a government installation like this is never as easy as it seems."

"How would you know that?" Joseph asked.

"I work for a contractor that helps rebuild infrastructure in recovering war zones. I've seen more than my fair share of military bases in the middle east," Don said.

Her father was right. He had a much better idea of what they might be dealing with than she did. "Dad, how would you get out of here?" she asked.

"I wouldn't. I'd sit tight and pray for it all to end quickly and well," he said bluntly.

She shook her head. "Not an option."

"It might have to be," Mark said. "It's not just us. We've got babies, and dogs, and a cat with us."

"Mark is right. There's no way we're all making it out of here safely," Don said.

As much as she didn't want to admit it, they had a point. Cindy took a deep breath. "Okay, so how do I get out of here?" she asked.

Her dad looked like he was about to say something, then hesitated.

"What?" she pushed.

He shook his head. "The best thing all of us can do right now is get some sleep, like the man said."

"There's no way I can sleep right now," Cindy said.

"Trust me, the adrenaline's going to wear off any minute now and then you're going to drop. You want to get out of here? Fine. I'll help you figure it out, but not until we've all had some sleep and can think more clearly. We're no good to Jeremiah or even ourselves if we collapse from exhaustion."

She knew her father was right. Something had been scratching at the corners of her mind for the last couple of minutes and her eyelids were starting to feel incredibly heavy. She was tired. She was certainly not capable of thinking straight at the moment and she would just manage to get herself caught or even injured if she attempted something rash in the state that she was in.

"Okay," she said finally.

"Good," Don said.

He turned and headed toward the beds. He grabbed one on the end which was closest to the door. The significance of his choice was not lost on her. He wanted to be the barrier between her and the outside, both to keep her safe from anything that came in and to keep her from trying to sneak out in the middle of the night. Given the way the beds were arranged it was mostly a symbolic gesture. She could easily get to the door without having to walk right past him.

Mark and Traci walked over and laid claim to two beds next to the cribs. Blackie walked over and jumped up on the end bed on the far side. He quickly curled up into a little ball.

"I guess my choice has been made for me," she said.

She walked over and sat down on the bed. Captain looked at the door and whined, and then after a moment came over and jumped up on the foot of her bed and lied down next to Blackie.

"I miss him, too, Cap," she told the dog as she stroked his head.

The others started getting ready for bed. She kept petting Captain, trying to let her mind zone out. It was hard, though. Her body was crashing but her mind kept flitting from one thought to the next, only alighting on each for a second before moving on again.

After a couple of minutes Geanie came and sat down on the bed next to hers. "Are you okay?"

"No," Cindy said. "Big surprise, right? Like it's not obvious that I'm a complete basket case."

Geanie reached out and touched her arm. "You're handling this unbelievably well. I don't think I'd be half as brave if I was in your shoes."

"Thanks, but I'm sure you'd be just fine," Cindy said.

"In the morning, we'll all put our heads together and figure out how to clear Jeremiah's name," she said.

Cindy could feel tears suddenly stinging her eyes. "Thank you, that would mean a lot," she said, her voice shaking.

"He's important to all of us, you know," Geanie said. "Well, maybe not to your mother," she said with a tiny smile.

Cindy smiled back. "It shouldn't be funny."

"But it kind of is," Geanie said.

Cindy nodded.

"See, with all of us thinking, we're sure to get this sorted out," Geanie said.

"I'll get Martin to help, too," Cindy said.

"Do you think he will?"

"I won't give him a choice."

~

Jeremiah rose with the dawn. He hadn't slept as much as he would have liked, but he had work to do and no time to waste.

He had just scraps of clues to work with as to who he was dealing with. He knew that the terrorist he had killed at Geanie and Joseph's wedding was one of them. He also knew that they had killed the Iranian student who wasn't willing to go along with his brothers' terror plot. He also knew that they had killed Captain's former owner because the man had been a witness to that. One of their members had also thrown the envelope that bore his nickname into Cindy's car.

He thought back to the wedding, to the man who had been trying to kill Cindy. Before Jeremiah had killed him he had said that his brothers would come for Jeremiah. He remembered clearly trying to find out who the man was.

"Who are you?"

"You do not recognize me?" the man asked.

He hadn't recognized him.

"Of course, how could you?" the man said. *"You never look to the left or the right."*

He still didn't know what that meant. All he knew was that a man he did not recognize had been willing to kill Cindy to get to him because of something he'd done in his past.

The list of potential enemies was long, but he had to ask himself which small group of people would devote time looking to hunt him down? That list would be much smaller.

They had taken their time coming forward despite several opportunities. Was it because they were too busy with whatever scheme they were hatching that Martin's people were trying to stop? Or was it because they weren't local and only passed through the area occasionally?

Someone had framed him for Not Paul's murder by planting that Barrett sniper rifle in his house. Given that the first known appearance of the men who were hunting him was a year later it seemed odd that they would have access to that information. In fact, outside the autopsy and police reports there should be no way they could have discovered what Not Paul was killed with.

Initially he'd thought the terrorists were the ones framing him for Not Paul's murder and Pastor Ben's. He figured they had wanted him exposed, vulnerable, and perhaps to destroy the trappings of his life before actually ending it.

However, that didn't completely add up. It made sense for them to try and frame him for Peter's murder and to expose the fact that he had killed their fallen comrade. They were in a position to know the details of both situations. It also was pretty common knowledge that he and Pastor Ben deeply disliked each other. Killing him and pinning that on Jeremiah would have been simple.

Not Paul, though, didn't make sense. There were so many other murders they could have tried to frame him for, ones where the information would have been more readily available. Something about it felt wrong. But who else could possibly want to frame him for murder and why?

Maybe he was going about this the wrong way. Maybe instead he needed to take a look at the murders that he and Cindy had solved and figure out if someone connected to one of them had the wherewithal and the motivation to destroy him.

In his head he tried to run it down. The serial killer from their first mystery together was dead and had no known family or anyone else to mourn him or attempt to avenge his death. The crooked cop who had been murdering the homeless and stealing their dogs was in jail. He wouldn't have had access to the police records of what happened almost four months later.

Frank Butler was the man who had hired the assassins who killed Not Paul. Pinning that murder instead on Jeremiah wouldn't much help him, though, given the other crimes he had committed and the fact that he'd cut a good deal with the district attorney in exchange for not pressing charges against Mark and the Pine Springs police force.

One by one he went through and dismissed possibilities. He kept coming back to Detective Keenan. He could think of no possible reason why the detective would have a grudge against him. He had seemed incredibly zealous the day before, though, like putting Jeremiah away was some personal vendetta.

He should do some digging into Keenan including his background and associates. Maybe it would shed a little light on things. He should also try to figure out what evidence Keenan had that convinced a judge to issue a warrant to search Jeremiah's home. As far as he'd been able to tell, the Barrett they'd found in his house had been the only thing pointing the finger at him. To get the warrant there had to be something else. There couldn't have been an eyewitness, but what if someone had lied and said they had witnessed the event or overheard Jeremiah confessing to it?

Since he hadn't been home when the warrant was executed, and Keenan hadn't shown it to him at the police station he didn't know what was in it. Now that he had gone dark it was going to be nearly impossible for him to get a look at it. Since Martin had Mark in protective custody along with all the others he couldn't get help from him in obtaining a copy.

That left him with three possibilities. He could try and get Liam to help. Given the position Liam had been placed in that would be tricky. Plus, he wanted to save interacting with Liam as a matter of last resort. He would only get one shot at playing that card and he needed to make it count.

He could reach out to Joseph's attorney. No one knew yet that Jeremiah had gone off the grid, so the request would seem fairly standard. While he had a burner phone, risking the contact either in person or by phone wasn't a great option. The less of a footprint he could leave the better.

The third option was to get it directly from the police precinct. It was a tricky proposition, but he knew that there were ways he could get in and get out undetected as long as he was quick. In order to facilitate it he would have to break a couple of laws, but what was it they said? In for a penny, in for a pound.

He had two problems: terrorists from his past were after him and someone was trying to frame him for murder. Until he could determine otherwise his best bet was to treat them as two different things and attack both head on.

Sneaking into the police precinct would have to wait for later in the day so it was time to start looking for the men who wanted him dead. While Los Angeles seemed a better place to look for terrorists, particularly those wanting to buy nasty weapons as Martin indicated, he was rarely in Los Angeles. The Iranian student had been killed in Pine Springs as had Peter, the former C.I.A. agent. The odds were excellent that Pine Springs was where they'd spotted Jeremiah as well since he rarely strayed outside of town. So, if he acted on the assumption that they were in or near Pine Springs then he had a few ideas where to start looking.

He flagged down a cab and had it drop him a quarter mile away from his ultimate destination. He would have preferred to "borrow" a car that wouldn't be likely to be reported missing for a while, but this would have to do for the time being. He was able to keep his hat low, shielding his face, and pay in cash. He was fairly certain as he walked away that the driver wouldn't know him from Adam if he saw him again.

Once on the street he kept his head down and walked purposefully. People who looked like they were headed somewhere were far less memorable than those who wandered slowly or looked around excessively. He turned down side streets three times just to make sure no one was following him.

He couldn't detect anyone watching him which was a relief. He didn't hasten, though. With these kind of missions too fast could be just as deadly as too slow when it came to making a move. When he'd found the building he was looking for, he walked around the block three times before being satisfied that no one in the area was even remotely interested in him.

Finally, he came to a stop on the sidewalk in front of his intended destination. A tiny shiver passed through him as he stared at the store in front of him. He couldn't help but feel déjà vu sweep over him. It had been a couple of years since he'd seen the place, but he'd never forget it.

He was staring at the check cashing business where the Passion Week killer had staged his version of Jesus driving the moneychangers from the Temple. And once again it looked like it had been the scene of a crime.

9

When Mark woke up it took him a few seconds to remember where he was. It was pitch black in the room, but there were a couple of night lights glowing in the two bathrooms. He sat up slowly, wondering how long he'd been asleep. Around him he could hear gentle snoring from at least three different people. It sounded like Traci was one of them. Her allergies must be acting up a bit.

He listened for sounds of movement, wondering if anyone else was awake yet. He desperately wished he could go back to sleep, but his brain was buzzing. It was Monday morning and they would miss him at work. He had a lot to do on his own cases and then he needed to be there to be an advocate for Jeremiah. If he was honest with himself that was going to be a lost cause once Keenan realized that Jeremiah had gone underground. Still, he would have liked to have spun it as long as he could. He trusted Liam to be fair, but he didn't trust Keenan to supply him with all the facts he needed.

He wondered what Liam would make of his disappearance. Of all their disappearances, actually. He had no idea how Martin thought he could explain the disappearance of more than a dozen people and animals.

"I need to get out of here," he whispered.

"How?" Cindy asked in his ear.

Mark jerked in surprise and barely suppressed a shout.

"Sorry," she whispered.

In the darkness he still couldn't see her, but apparently her eyes had adjusted already.

"Meet me at the table," she instructed.

He nodded.

He heard a whisper of movement as she left. She was getting as bad as Jeremiah about sneaking up on people. He turned his head away from the bathrooms and their nightlights and tried to pierce the rest of the darkness. It was then that he realized that there was a clock on the microwave shedding some light in that area. According to it the time was a quarter after ten. With no windows in the room he would have never guessed it was day already let alone that late.

He got up and shuffled slowly toward the microwave, knowing that the table was close by. When he was almost there he saw it. A shadowy figure that had to be Cindy was sitting at it already. He took a seat across from her. They were both bathed in the glow from the microwave clock. As far as meetings went it didn't get much more clandestine, he thought to himself.

"How long have you been up?" he whispered.

"A long time."

He refrained from asking her if that meant she hadn't slept at all yet. He didn't want to know because he didn't want to lecture her. That's what her dad was for. He couldn't deny that the urge was there, though.

"I'm turning into a dad."

"What?" she asked.

"Never mind. What's going on?"

"Nothing," she said, the frustration evident in her voice.

"No word from our friendly neighborhood spooks?" he asked.

"Not a one."

"You know, for Jeremiah to be free to do what he needs to do he can't be worried about what's happening to you. It would be better for him if you just stayed here, safe," he said, feeling like a hypocrite.

"I can't, for the same reason that I couldn't just stay behind when he went to Israel," she said.

"Because you want to know what happens if something happens."

"Yes."

He reached out and grabbed her hand and gave it a squeeze. "I'm sure he's going to be fine. This is, after all, his thing. It's what he's trained to do."

"You want out of here just as badly as I do," Cindy said.

"Yeah, because I want to do my thing, what I'm trained to do. I want to make sure that he has a life worth coming home to."

"Is this a private conversation or can anyone join?" Don asked from behind Mark.

Mark jumped again. "Dang it! I'm going to have to put bells on both of you," he said.

Don sat down next to him. "You know, I think we have everything we need right here to help Jeremiah."

"How?" Mark asked.

"Figure out who killed those four men."

"That's not entirely helpful since Jeremiah did kill one of them," Mark said then winced. "I'm sorry, I shouldn't have said-"

Don shook his head. "I'm under no illusions when it comes to my future son-in-law."

Cindy reached out with her free hand and grabbed her father's. For one second Mark thought he and Don should hold hands, too, then they could all sing a chorus of Kumbaya.

"Okay, I definitely need more sleep," he muttered.

"Don't we all. Okay, so what about the other three?"

"We already know who killed two of them. Terrorists killed one and a hired assassin killed the other."

"Then why is Jeremiah being accused?"

Mark shook his head. "Something strange is going on. I think someone is trying to set up Jeremiah."

"Okay, so we can work on figuring out the who, why, and how of that. What about the last?"

"Pastor Ben. That just happened, and I don't know much about it," Mark admitted.

"Is it possible that whoever killed him is also framing Jeremiah for the other murders?"

"Anything is possible. It just seems like a lot of work."

Even in the dim blue light Mark could see Don roll his eyes. "Have you never seen someone exact revenge before?"

His thoughts instantly went to the Passion Week killer who had been taking revenge in his own sick way on the friend who had wronged him. That man had gone to insane amounts of effort to make his point.

"I have and you're right," he admitted.

"Cindy and I walked around Ben's place," Don said.

"You, what? What did you do?"

"We checked out the crime scene," Cindy said.

"Oh, well, we have that," Mark said, not wanting to know how that had even come about.

"Maybe the best thing we can do is put together everything we know and solve the legal entanglement while Jeremiah handles the physical danger," Don said.

Before either Mark or Cindy could say anything, Blackie landed suddenly on the table in front of him.

"For the love of all that's holy!" Mark exclaimed.

"Ssh! You're going to wake everyone else up," Cindy said as she scooped the cat into her arms.

"Too late," Traci said as she turned on a lamp on one of the nightstands.

Rachel began to cry.

"Now we've done it," Mark said.

"I thought it was all a nightmare!" Carol wailed.

"Tell me about it," Don muttered.

~

Jeremiah approached the check cashing building cautiously. There was yellow police tape around the building. There were no smashed windows or obvious external signs of a problem other than the tape itself. He slipped on a pair of gloves as he walked, another item he had "borrowed" from Joseph before leaving his house.

There was no one nearby. The parking lot of the church next door was empty. Once he was certain no one could see him he slipped under the tape. It took seconds to pick the lock on the door and then he was inside.

He looked around. It still wasn't immediately obvious what the problem was until he noticed that the lock on the door that led into the employee part of the building had been shot out.

He pushed the door open and walked into the space. There, on the floor behind one of the three transaction windows, was a large bloodstain. There was a chalk outline of a body around it. He crouched down to get a better look at it. Whoever had been shot had been just under six feet tall. The bloodstain was in the region of the abdomen.

He stood up and inspected the counter and the glass. The glass was bullet proof and was intact. Whoever shot the man had done so through the slot at the bottom through which money and documents were passed. In order to pull it off they would have had to do so swiftly, before the teller could move away. If his killer had been on the other side of the glass when he shot him, though, then why had he shot the lock on the door? He could have wanted to make sure that his victim actually died from his injury. There was no second blood stain evident on the ground, though.

Jeremiah checked the cash drawers and there was money still in them. Robbery couldn't have been the killer's motive. If they weren't here because they wanted money then they were likely here because they were sending money. He himself had come here to find out if foreign nationals had been using the place to send money home. Looks like he had his answer.

A trash can in the center of the floor caught his attention. It wasn't in a logical place, but was pulled out slightly. He walked over to it. There were charred remains of some documents inside. He bent down and sifted through them. Depending on how much time the killer thought he had before the police arrived he might not have stuck around to make sure that everything burned completely.

At last he found a couple of scraps of paper that were still somewhat intact even though they were blackened. He looked around until he found a wire basket used to hold papers. He emptied it then placed the charred paper in the basket. He pulled a matchbook out of his pocket and lit a match which he then held under the basket.

The flame came up and for a moment the words on the charred paper flared to life. It was a money transfer to somewhere in Iran and the name of the transferee was Ashkan Shirazi. The name didn't mean anything to him, but then he hadn't expected that it would be a name he recognized. That would have been too easy. Still, it was something.

He dropped the paper and the match back into the trashcan. He had a name, but he wanted more than that. He wanted an address or a picture.

If Shirazi was indeed one of the terrorists who had been operating in the area, then it was possible that he had been to this business before to send money overseas or receive money. Which meant there were probably other records.

In the back office he found a computer that was still on. He didn't know if the police had already searched it, but if they had missed the charred document in the trashcan then they might not have known who they were looking for.

It took him a couple of minutes, but he finally found what he wanted. Shirazi had come in six times over the past twelve months. An address for an apartment was listed on his profile. His most recent transaction that had been logged was ten days earlier.

The police had undoubtedly confiscated the security footage for the time of the murder, but he doubted they'd gone that far back. He found the backup discs after a little searching in the office and grabbed the one for the day he was looking for. He popped it into the computer and started playing it ten minutes before the timestamp for Shirazi's transaction.

When Shirazi appeared on camera, Jeremiah sighed in frustration. The man had been wearing a baseball cap and kept his head down, never letting the camera get a good look at his face. He kept watching, hoping to see something that would help him. Shirazi was right-handed, he noticed, and roughly average height. Nothing he was seeing on the security footage would help him pick the man out of a crowd.

Suddenly a man stepped forward into frame. Shirazi turned his head, clearly speaking to him, then handed him something. The man turned around but before he stepped out of frame there was a moment where Jeremiah could see his face clear as day.

He smiled. He might not know what Shirazi looked like, but he had an address and knew what one of the man's associates looked like. It was more than enough.

As he began to put everything back just the way he'd found it he debated whether to go after Shirazi now or to prep for sneaking into the police precinct. He finally opted for going after Shirazi. Even if the terrorists weren't responsible for framing him it was the best use of time. After all, as far as the police were concerned he shouldn't be missing just yet. If he could handle Shirazi and his friends fast then he could devote all the rest of his time to fixing his other problem.

He was about to exit the building when a sudden uneasy feeling settled over him. He hesitated and was about to peer out the windows when something told him to back away.

It was not the first time he'd had that feeling in the field. He never knew whether he heard something so faint it didn't really register or saw a flicker of movement or if

G-d was just giving him a warning. He knew better than to ignore it, whatever it was.

He retreated back and then kept going farther until he was back in the office. He didn't like it because there was no way out back there. A business like this should have an extra escape route, but it didn't.

He crouched down against the wall next to the door and did his best to calm his breathing and slow his heart. He needed to focus. He strained his ears, closing his eyes so that he could hear better.

The front door of the business opened and then closed. The length of time between the two made him think two people entered instead of just one. He listened for footsteps, but didn't hear any for several moments. Whoever was out there was concerned about being caught. If it was a police officer coming back to check something regarding the scene they would have walked with strong steps. If it was just looters seeing an opportunity they would have been louder, faster, possibly agitated. He heard a step and then moments later another. Whoever was out there was moving slowly, quietly.

He heard the door that separated the customers from the employees open. Now he could clearly make out footfalls, soft though they were. There were definitely two sets.

"See, the fire took care of it," a heavily accented voice said.

He would bet the man was from Iran and hadn't been in the United States for more than a few months. He waited for the second person to speak, but they didn't. Instead the first man spoke again.

"What's wrong?"

There was a lengthy pause. Finally, a second male voice spoke. He had the same accent, but it wasn't as heavy, and he spoke English with more practiced ease. "It's warm. Someone set fire to these again, recently."

"There's no one here, just us," the first man said.

If he had to guess he would say the second man could be Shirazi. The man was more cautious than his companion.

Jeremiah heard the sound of a gun being unholstered.

"Where are you going?" the first man asked.

Even though there was no answer, Jeremiah knew exactly where the other man was going. He was coming for the back office where Jeremiah was.

He was trapped with no way out.

10

Jeremiah's muscles coiled. With two of them out there his position was far from ideal. Given that one of them was expecting trouble made it that much worse. Further complicating matters was that he needed to keep one alive to interrogate. He waited. He'd have a split second where he had the upper hand and he'd have to make the most of it.

The footsteps suddenly stopped.

They were in a stalemate. The man with the gun was clearly reasonably certain that Jeremiah was there. Jeremiah slid to the floor and rolled as far from the door as he could. A second later a bullet came through the wall by the door exactly where he had been.

He could choose to make a sound like someone being hit and falling down or remain absolutely silent. He opted for the latter, not wanting to risk the man shooting again.

The gunman spoke in Persian to the other man, telling him to go check it out. The gunman felt his companion was expendable else he wouldn't have sent him at that moment.

Jeremiah rose silently to his feet and pulled out his gun. The other man came through the door. Jeremiah recognized him as the man from the security video and leaped at him. He spun him around and locked his left arm around the man's throat. Using him as a shield he shoved the man forward into the doorway and fired at the gunman who returned fire a split second later.

Jeremiah's bullet hit the gunman in his right shoulder and he dropped the gun. His bullet hit his comrade in the forehead and the man slumped. Jeremiah let the body drop and leaped over it to kick the other man in the side of the knee. He went down, and Jeremiah grabbed his left arm, pulled it out, kicked him hard in the armpit to dislocate his shoulder, then dropped his full weight on it to shatter it.

The man screamed in agony as he writhed beneath him. Jeremiah stood up, took the man's gun and removed the clip before tossing it into the back room. He put away his own gun and looked down at the man on the ground.

"Ashkan Shirazi, I presume."

The man glared up at him but said nothing.

Jeremiah looked him in the eyes. "We're both professionals and so we both know that eventually everyone talks."

"Not everyone has something to say," Shirazi said.

"But I'm pretty sure you do. Now, we can spend hours, days even, going round and round. I can torture you. You can refuse to talk. I can torture you some more. You can tell me lies thinking I'll believe them. I can torture you more. Eventually you will tell me what I want to know."

"And what is it you want to know?"

"The truth."

"Since when is *malakh ha-mavet* interested in the truth? All the angel of death wishes is to kill."

Jeremiah crouched down. "You want to see the angel of death?" he asked, letting menace fill his voice.

The other man's eyes widened in fear.

Jeremiah sneered. "I didn't think so. How about you tell me what I want to know, and you don't have to see the angel of death."

"One does not have to see him to be struck down by him."

Jeremiah chuckled. "True."

He brought his knee down on the man's shattered shoulder, applying pressure. Shirazi screamed and nearly fainted. Jeremiah eased up and slapped him across the face. "Stay with me. You don't want to pass out with wounds like yours. You'd never wake up."

"I'm dead anyway," the man gasped.

"Answer my questions and I'll consider letting you get to a hospital in time."

"What do you want to know?"

"How many of you are there?"

"Many."

Jeremiah dropped his knee onto Shirazi's shoulder for a moment then lifted it back up.

"Five still besides me."

"Who else have you told about me being here?"

Shirazi glared in defiance. Jeremiah raised an eyebrow.

"Everyone."

Jeremiah slammed his knee down hard.

"No one! No one else!"

"Why do you want me dead?"

"You never look to the left or the right."

"One of yours said that to me over a year ago. What does it mean?"

Shirazi's eyes started to roll back in his head and Jeremiah slapped him again. "Stay with me!"

"You only look at those you kill," the man said, slurring his words.

~

"I can't remember the last time I had Froot Loops," Don said as they all sat at the table with bowls of cereal.

"I'd forgotten how good they are," Mark said.

"You'll have plenty of time to remember when the twins get a little older," Geanie said.

"We're not feeding them this kind of stuff," Mark said.

Traci rolled her eyes at him. "Speak for yourself."

"What? What about living healthy?" he asked.

"Says the man who won't be the one responsible for all the meals," Traci said.

Geanie tried to suppress a laugh and it squeaked out anyway which set Joseph and Don off.

The only three who were quiet were Cindy, Carol and Kyle. Her mother and brother weren't eating with the rest of them. They were sitting apart and looked more miserable than she could remember seeing them in a very long time. Cindy was fixated on escaping and trying her best to ignore the throbbing pain in her broken arm that the painkillers weren't making a dent in.

She was glad that her friends were able to make the best of a bad situation, but she couldn't stop herself from thinking that Jeremiah was out there alone, and anything could be happening to him.

Over the past few years God had brought her and Jeremiah through so many things without any lasting damage. They'd been living charmed lives in that regard, as had their friends. She looked around the table and thought about all the times and ways one of them could have been permanently injured or killed.

As a cop Mark put himself on the line every day. He got shot at and his former partner had been killed and his current partner badly injured. She remembered when Mark had been poisoned and she had thought he was dying. The doctors had said he was lucky to be alive.

Geanie had been nearly killed by the psychopath who wanted to marry Joseph. Joseph himself had been poisoned during all that craziness and nearly killed.

Kyle had nearly been killed when his fiancée had been targeted. Kyle himself had also been the target of a murderer on the cattle drive. And that had put Jeremiah, her, Mark, and Traci in danger as well.

Traci had been kidnapped by the men who had killed several homeless people. They could easily have killed her, too.

Cindy herself was no stranger to kidnapping and there were so many times when she had thought she was going to be killed. Most recently when Leo had been killed in her home and the ambulance she was in after had been attacked. Her broken arm was a stark reminder of those events.

It was a miracle that they had all come through so much alive and in one piece. And as much as she didn't want to let the fear creep in, she sometimes couldn't help but wonder if it was just a matter of time before one of them was killed.

She looked around the table again, thinking about how each person there had impacted her life. She wasn't ready to lose them.

"You don't look okay, honey," her dad said to her.

She jumped, startled.

"I'm not," she muttered.

"Jeremiah is a resourceful man," he said, leaning over and giving her hand a squeeze.

"I know," she said.

"I wonder how long we're going to be here?" Traci said.

"I've been thinking about that, too," Geanie chimed in. "I'm worried that we're going to miss Pastor Ben's funeral."

Cindy grimaced and mentally kicked herself for not having thought much about that or him. She felt a bit guilty for not having shed any tears for him. The truth was, though, that they hadn't been close, they hadn't known each other overly long, and he had made her life more difficult than not.

"I never really liked him," Joseph admitted. "I know that sounds bad, particularly considering..."

"I'm glad you said it first," Geanie said. "Honestly, I think the only one on staff who's really going to miss him is Dave."

"Wildman?" Mark asked.

"Yeah. He was thrilled that Pastor Ben approved having a Halloween event for the first time ever," Cindy said.

"That was something," Mark said.

"Some of the parishioners will miss him," Joseph said. "He was a decent preacher and he was really good about visitations. Better than Roy was."

"Most of the time when Roy was there I did the visitations because he just wouldn't," Cindy said.

"I know," Geanie said. "So, while we might not have liked him personally, it is a loss for the church. I just wish we could be there to be supportive."

"I'm still trying to figure out what Martin's telling them about why we all disappeared," Joseph said with a sigh.

"Sometimes I feel like my life gets in the way of my life," Cindy said, her frustration boiling over.

"What does that mean?" Traci asked. There was no judgment in her eyes, just curiosity.

"I feel like I get shot at, kidnapped, and have to spend so much time dealing with bodies and police officers that I should be a cop and not a church secretary," Cindy confided. "Sometimes I think I'm falling down at the job I get paid to do."

"You do a ton at work. And we already established that you are irreplaceable," Geanie said fervently.

"Yeah, but I could do better. I used to do better."

"But now you *are* better," Joseph pointed out. "You're a better, more rounded person. You are warmer in your interactions with people and they've noticed."

"They have?" Cindy asked, startled.

Joseph nodded. "It wasn't just Geanie and I demanding that you come back to the church you know. And I'm not talking about Dave and Sylvia. Lots of members came forward. They didn't know the circumstances. Ben even pointed out how many sick days you'd had to take because of other things you were involved in. People were adamant that they'd rather have you part time than anyone else full time."

"Really?" Cindy asked, stunned.

Joseph nodded. "Plus, a lot of them love the fact that they can tell their friends that their church secretary is a famous crime solver."

"They did not!" Cindy burst out.

Joseph smirked. "At least a dozen did. And none of them are in this room."

"Sometimes we never know the impact we have on other people," Geanie said, smiling at her.

"Well, clearly I didn't," Cindy muttered. She took a deep breath. "Okay, as the resident church crime solver it falls to me to figure out who killed Ben."

"It falls to us," Traci corrected. "We're your posse."

"Hey, I don't have a posse," Mark protested.

Traci rolled her eyes. "No, you just have an entire police force."

"Yeah, but not all of them like me."

"Boo hoo," Traci said.

Mark ended up with such a look of mock hurt on his face that Cindy actually started laughing out loud.

"That's what I like to hear," her dad said, beaming.

Her agitation and frustration eased up as she realized that she wasn't helpless sitting in this room. She could and would solve the mystery of what had happened to Ben so that when Jeremiah walked through the door they'd have one less problem to worry about. She looked around affectionately at those around her. They really were like her posse, always there for her, always willing to help her hunt down the bad guys. And, in the case of Traci and Mark, they had actually even ridden together. In that moment she realized, perhaps for the first time, just how lucky she was, how blessed she was to have all these people to stand by her. She wasn't alone and that was the best feeling in the world.

"Okay, posse, everyone saddle up. We've got some outlaws to bust," she said with a grin.

"Yee-haw!" Joseph yelled suddenly making them all laugh until they cried.

Jeremiah was almost finished with the man he was interrogating. The guy was fading, and he didn't have much time left to try and get information out of him. He'd bled quite a lot from the bullet wound in his shoulder and the pain from his other shoulder had taken its toll.

"Stay with me," Jeremiah commanded as the man looked like he might pass out. "The other five men besides you, where can I find them?" Jeremiah asked.

"I don't know. I swear. We've been meeting once a week. We don't know where each is in case of this," Shirazi said.

Jeremiah believed that, frustrating as it was. He was certain he'd extricated as much information as he could from the man. He stood up and pulled out his gun.

"Wait! You said you'd consider letting me go to the hospital."

"I did consider it. And I decided, you really belong in the morgue," Jeremiah said.

He lifted the gun up, ready to aim at the man's head. When suddenly Shirazi smiled. Then he laughed. A chill went up Jeremiah's spine. He had missed something. Something vital. While he'd spent the last twelve hours figuring out how he was going to find them, they had spent the last twelve months figuring out how they were going to kill him. He thought he'd found the terrorists when in reality they had trapped him.

"You never look to the left or the right," Shirazi said.

In that moment Jeremiah realized that he was standing in between two bombs.

11

Mark was pleased at the direction things had taken. Cindy was on task now, focusing her energies on how they could clear Jeremiah's name instead of trying to formulate escape plans that at the best would be futile and at the worst deadly. It also felt really good to laugh for a while.

Sometimes life was too serious. Actually, it was that way far too often. He wanted to find ways to lighten the mood more often. Given his job he often saw the worst parts of society and human nature. It was good in his off-time to focus on the best parts. Looking around the table he realized that these people were the best parts. He didn't know how they'd all become like some sort of bizarre family, but they had.

He was grateful that Ryan and Rachel would grow up knowing these people and being influenced by them. And that wasn't just because he knew Joseph would buy them ponies.

He smiled at the thought.

"What scheme are you hatching?" Geanie asked, catching his expression.

"I was just thinking about the ponies you and Joseph are going to buy Ryan and Rachel," he said.

"Darn straight," Joseph said with a grin.

"Imagine if one of them grew up and went to the Olympics for the equestrian events!" Geanie said.

"One of them? Why not both of them?" Joseph said.

"I'm personally hoping for a musician," Traci said.

"A rock star?" Geanie asked.

"Or a violin virtuoso?" Joseph countered.

"I'd be happy if they can do Chopsticks on the piano," Mark said. "Course, I'm thinking Rachel will grow up to be Wonder Woman."

"*I'm* Wonder Woman," Traci said, taking mock offense.

"You certainly are," Cindy reassured her.

"Thank you," Traci said pertly.

"How about Princess Leia?" Joseph asked. "Still royalty and a warrior and a great leader."

"Does that make Ryan Luke then?" Geanie asked.

"Oh no, I don't need either of my kids force choking me when they don't want to eat peas and carrots," Mark said emphatically.

"Darth Mark, I'll never rule the galaxy with you," Joseph said, brandishing his spoon like it was a lightsaber.

Mark couldn't help himself. He hit Joseph's spoon with his own. "Joseph, I am your father," he said in his deepest voice.

Traci had taken a sip of water and ended up spitting it all over Geanie as she started laughing.

Joseph leaped to his feet. "Hello, my name is Joseph Coulter, your wife has spit water on my wife. Prepare to die." He brandished the spoon anew.

Mark got up. "Why am I always the villain?" he asked, holding his own spoon aloft.

"If you have to ask-" Joseph said with a smirk.

Mark crossed spoons with the other man and they both took up fighting stances.

"See, I'm thinking the twins could be the greatest Olympic fencers the world has ever seen," Joseph said.

"Why do you guys keep picking rich people sports?" Mark asked.

Joseph raised an eyebrow. "Um, because when it comes to the Olympics they're pretty much all rich people sports. You know how much money all of those athletes have to raise for training, competition, travel, equipment, all of it?"

"See, this is why Ryan's going to develop a love for football, play in high school, hopefully get a scholarship for college, you know something I can afford," Mark said.

Joseph lowered his spoon suddenly and had a stricken look on his face. "You're kidding me, right?"

Mark lowered his spoon, wondering why the other man was looking at him that way. "What?" he asked. "I don't make a lot of money, so I'm hoping they're both smart enough or talented enough or both to help pay for college."

Joseph looked at Geanie who was still drying the water off herself. She caught Joseph's look and shrugged.

Joseph turned back. "Mark, we told you we set up college funds for them when they were born, right?"

"Yes, and we appreciate that so much, but college gets expensive, and with inflation, I worry."

Joseph shook his head. He stepped forward and gripped Mark's shoulder. "You don't have to worry about Ryan and Rachel ever."

"That's sweet, but-"

"But nothing. We set up a million-dollar trust fund for each of them the day after they were born."

Mark was flabbergasted. He stared at Joseph and had no idea what to say. He finally turned to Geanie who just nodded. Traci had tears running down her cheeks as she leaned across the table and hugged Geanie.

He turned back to Joseph and hugged him. "Thank you," he said.

"You're welcome. We don't have a lot in the way of blood family, but you guys are our family."

Mark pulled away and cleared his throat. "There's something Traci and I have been wanting to ask you. We want to put you guys down in our will as Ryan and Rachel's guardians if anything were to happen to us."

It was Joseph's turn to grab him and hug him tight. Mark could barely breathe, and he was surprised at the amount of emotion he felt coming off the other man.

"We'd be honored," Geanie said.

Mark pulled away and wiped his eyes. "Okay, that is officially enough crying for today."

"I agree," Geanie said, her voice chipper, but with a slight edge to it.

"Spoon truce?" Joseph said, holding up his weapon.

"Spoon truce. For now," Mark said with a grin.

"How about you mighty warriors clean up the dishes since you're already up?" Traci suggested.

Mark groaned. "Dishes? But we just had a moment."

"You'll have an entirely different kind of moment if you think us girls are doing it," Traci said tartly.

"Yes, Dear," Mark said.

Don chuckled. "The two most powerful words in the English language."

Mark couldn't help glance over at Don's wife and son who were keeping to themselves. He didn't want to even guess at how that relationship worked.

~

"Good call on dishes," Cindy said as Mark and Joseph got to work. "There's not that much to clean up, though."

"Oh, don't worry. We're not taking turns," Traci said. "Mark's here with us 24/7 so he has plenty of dishes to make up for."

Cindy couldn't help but smile at that even as she desperately wished that Jeremiah was there with them. She looked at her dad who was staring at her intently. He gave her a little nod, as though acknowledging that he knew what she was thinking.

She glanced over at her mother and brother. Part of her felt bad that they were isolated, but she reminded herself that they had chosen that. They could have eaten with the rest of them like her father. That would mean supporting her in some way, though, and maybe they just weren't capable of it. She wasn't surprised by her mom, but she'd expected a little more from Kyle, especially after all the effort she'd gone through to try and connect with him more.

"Wishing you had your extra special dartboard?" her dad asked.

"How did you know about that?" she asked, eyes wide.

He chuckled. "I saw it the last time we visited you a few years back. I actually thought it was funny. You've gotten really good at darts."

"It actually saved my life two years ago," she said.

"Really? Now that's a story I'd like to hear more about."

She smiled. While she tried to tell her parents about her adventures, she knew that her mother didn't always seem to care and probably didn't share everything. Cindy also managed to keep most of the really scary stuff under wraps.

Maybe that had been a mistake. Their mom worshipped Kyle and he did dangerous stuff all the time.

She lowered her voice. "This awful bad guy and his buddies cornered me in an Irish pub."

Don cocked his head to the side. "I remember something about St. Patrick's Day and catching bad guys at a pub, but I don't think I heard anything about darts."

She nodded. "Well, they had me trapped and they were going to kill me. I grabbed darts out of a dartboard and was trying to threaten them, so I could get to the door and escape."

"And they underestimated you?"

She nodded. "I hit some guys in the face," she said.

"Wow! I'm impressed. A bit scared that it happened in the first place, but definitely proud."

"Thank you," she said, glowing at the praise.

He smiled at her. "A lot of people underestimate you."

"Tell me about it," she said, glancing at her mom and Kyle.

He reached out and grabbed her hand. "I know it's frustrating, but you can use that to your advantage."

"I never thought about it that way," she admitted.

"I know. You're an amazing woman and I'm very, very happy to see that you're not as afraid of the world as you were for so long."

She nodded. "Jeremiah was a big part of that."

"I know. So were they," he said, indicating the others there. "You've made some amazing friends. I hope you treasure them."

"I do."

"Good. Now enough serious talk."

"Well, we should get to work on solving Ben's murder," she said.

"In a bit. I had something else in mind for right now."

"Oh, what's that?" she asked.

"Who's up for a game of Clue?" he said loudly.

"Ooh, me!" Geanie squeaked, raising her hand.

"She loves games," Joseph said, turning from the sink with a laugh.

"Oh, and you don't," Geanie said, sticking her tongue out at him.

"Of course I do, but compared to you I'm an amateur."

"Yeah, well, I think I can whoop all of you crime solvers with one eye closed," Don said.

"Challenge accepted!" Geanie shouted.

Cindy had to laugh at her friend. A moment later, though, she said, "But we have important work to do."

"Yes," Don said, "and we're all still exhausted. Playing the game will help stimulate our creative juices. It will be fun and therapeutic as well as an excellent warm up."

"I never would have thought about it that way," Cindy admitted.

"That's why you need your dad," he said with a grin.

"I piled the games on the floor over there," Traci said, pointing.

"I'll go get it," Cindy said. She stood up and stretched. Maybe her dad was right. Some downtime would probably go a long way to helping them all recuperate a bit and tackle things fresh.

She turned and walked toward the games. She loved Clue. She and her dad and Lisa used to play it a lot when she was little. She eyed the other games. Maybe after Clue they could play-

A sudden wave of terror washed over Cindy, so intense that she actually screamed out loud and collapsed onto the floor. Everyone ran to her.

"What's wrong?" Mark was the first to ask.

"Jeremiah," she panted. "Jeremiah."

She couldn't get any other words out to explain what she was feeling. All she knew was that something terrible was happening to him. She began to sob in fear and pain.

Geanie dropped next to her and grabbed her hand. "God, we ask for your protection over Jeremiah right now," she began in a strong, clear voice. "You've protected him more times than I can count. You've protected us all. Please God, watch over him, bring him safely through this and home to us quickly."

Geanie's voice started to shake as Joseph sat down and grabbed her hand. "Father, heal whatever needs healing. Give him strength, courage, and wisdom to see what path to take."

Traci sat down and grabbed Cindy's other hand, holding it gently. "God, help him. Help us."

Cindy's father joined the circle and began to pray in a deep, calm voice.

~

Mark could feel panic taking hold of him. He felt completely and utterly helpless. He wanted to throw himself at the door, demand that the agents outside release him so that he could go help his best friend, his brother.

He felt eyes on him and he turned and saw Traci looking up at him. He walked to her. She reached up her free hand to him and nodded. He took it and she tugged him down next to her. Don grabbed his other hand in a firm grip. And just like that he was part of the circle.

"Save him, please," the words burst out of him. Tears started streaming down his face. Traci squeezed his hand hard and he clung to her and Don as he began to shake.

For just a moment it was as though he could feel the emotions of everyone else in the circle, their pain, their fear, and then, their hope and their resolve. A strange sense of peace settled over him. He was still afraid for Jeremiah, but something deep down told him that whatever happened, they would get through it.

Around him the others continued to pray, sometimes in short bursts, other times lengthier. He didn't speak again, just sat and tried to breathe deeply, not ready to understand what was happening but grateful that it was.

He didn't know how long they sat there. It could have been minutes or hours. He lost all sense of time.

Suddenly he heard a door open.

They all stopped, turned and looked. Martin stood just inside the door. "Everyone okay?" he asked, his brow furrowed,

Cindy leaped to her feet. "What's happened to Jeremiah?" she demanded.

"How did you know something happened?" Martin asked sharply.

Mark felt like he was going to be sick as he stood up. He moved next to Cindy, sensing that something terrible was about to happen.

Cindy walked forward until she was standing inches from Martin. Mark walked with her but held back slightly so he could watch both of them. Behind him he could feel the tension coming off everyone else in the room. It was like the whole world was holding its breath, waiting.

"What happened?" Cindy said, her voice clear and ringing.

"We're not sure yet," Martin said. "There was a bomb blast."

"And?" she said.

"We've got people going through the rubble."

Martin looked like he wanted to be anywhere but right there. Mark recognized the look. It was how cops felt when they had to deliver the worst news any loved one could get. He felt a lump form in his throat as tears stung his eyes.

"Have you found him?"

Martin shook his head.

"But you found something," Cindy said.

Martin nodded. "I'm sorry. It's not good. The place was reduced mostly to ash. There's not much that's going to be found. We're going to have to check for bone particles. But we did find-" He sighed and dropped his eyes. "Cindy, I'm so sorry. We found two of Jeremiah's fingers."

12

"It doesn't mean he's dead," Mark half-shouted before anyone else could react.

Martin gave him a look that said otherwise, but he refused to believe it. The C.I.A. agent didn't know Jeremiah like he did. The man was a survivor.

Traci and Geanie both began to cry. They reached out to Cindy, but she shook off their hands. She stepped even closer to Martin.

"This had better not be another trick like last time," she hissed.

Martin shook his head. "It's not, Cindy. There's nothing to be gained here. And you know I was against leaving you in the dark overseas."

"Take me there right now," she said, fury in her voice.

"I can't do that."

"The hell you can't. You're C.I.A.. You can, and you will."

"It's complicated."

"Then let me make it simple for you. Either you take me there right now or when I get out of here I'll go to the press with what really happened in Jerusalem."

"You took an oath of secrecy," Martin said.

"Do I look like I care?" Cindy asked.

"She doesn't," Mark spoke up. "Trust me, last time I saw her like this Jeremiah had to end up taking her to Jerusalem with him."

Martin lowered his voice. "I like you, Cindy, I really do, but don't force my hand. Neither of us will like where that leads."

"You owe me."

"If Jeremiah is still alive then it's still too dangerous for you to be out there."

"And if he's not then you're going to have to let me go anyway. And, you think he's dead, so…"

Mark could tell she'd backed the man into a corner. Just when he thought that Martin was going to cave, he instead turned on his heel and left. The door closed and locked firmly behind him.

Cindy let out a scream of frustration.

"You did your best," he said quietly.

"Oh, I'm not done yet," she said, turning around. "I'm going to get out of here one way or another."

"Given that he's dead the nightmare is over. Shouldn't they let us go now?" Carol asked.

Mark winced. He was pretty sure that she hadn't meant it the way it came out. At least, he really hoped for her sake that she hadn't. He braced himself for what was going to happen next.

The explosion came, but from a different direction than he had expected. Traci took an angry step toward Carol. "How dare you say that about him? He was a hero and our friend!"

"I didn't mean it that way," Carol snapped. "But he was hardly a hero. He was a common murderer."

Traci moved like lightning, and before anyone could stop her, she slapped Carol as hard as she could. Kyle leaped forward to defend his mom, and Traci spun and punched him in the eye. He howled in pain.

Mark had never seen such violence from his wife and he stared in shock, rooted to the ground. Joseph reached her before anyone else could and he pulled Traci into a fierce hug. She collapsed against him sobbing as Geanie hovered nearby, glaring daggers at Carol and Kyle.

Carol spun toward her husband. "Are you going to let them do that?" she demanded.

He grimaced. "Frankly, you're lucky it wasn't your daughter who did that," he said.

"Her?" Carol scoffed, waving toward Cindy. "She's scared of her own shadow. Not like-"

She stopped speaking suddenly but Mark had a feeling she had been about to compare Cindy to Kyle. Or worse, to her dead sister, Lisa.

Don looked pained. "I know you stopped paying attention a long time ago, but you really should see the person Cindy's become. She's remarkable."

"She's stupid. She's planning to marry some idiot with no money, no prospects, and who would have spent his life in prison if he hadn't been killed!" Carol yelled.

It was like watching a car crash and being helpless to do anything to stop it.

"You take that back! All of it," Geanie shouted.

Ryan and Rachel both started crying. He should go to them. He should stop the fighting. He should do something. A decade and a half as a cop and he'd never frozen in the face of danger before. Now he just stared, horrified, as violence was erupting around him. And all he could think over and over was that Jeremiah couldn't be dead.

"I'm glad he's dead!" Kyle shouted, still clutching his eye.

Traci turned, jumped out of Joseph's arms, and knocked Kyle to the ground. She straddled him and began hitting him some more. Don and Joseph shouted, surging forward to try and break it up while Geanie screamed at Traci to hit him some more.

Suddenly two big guys in dark suits shoved past him. One of them wrapped his arms around Traci's waist and literally picked her up in the air, peeling her off of Kyle. The other barked at Kyle to stay down as he got between Geanie and Kyle.

Everyone was shouting louder. The babies were screaming now. Don and Joseph were urging calm, but had to yell to make themselves heard. Geanie and Traci were out for blood. Kyle and Carol were both ranting like lunatics. And he was just standing there watching. And Cindy...

He turned his head with a frown. Cindy was...

He spun around and saw the open door behind him. Cindy was gone.

~

Jeremiah was in trouble. He'd barely made it out of the exploding building with his life. As it was his collarbone on the left side was broken and the pain was overwhelming. Most of his left arm was useless because of it. He'd managed to wrap up his hand and get the bleeding stopped from the two severed fingers.

He was holed up in the men's room of the church next door to the check cashing place. He'd managed to get in there and he'd used the sink and a first aid kit he'd found to take care of himself as best he could. He had heard fire

114

trucks arrive on the scene. He waited until he could slip away without being spotted.

Part of him wanted nothing more than to go outside, have the firemen call an ambulance and go to a hospital. It would be tantamount to suicide, though.

The men who were after him had planned it all. It was possible they'd even murdered the teller as a way of getting his attention when they were ready. They couldn't have known that Mark and he were so busy with a different case that they wouldn't even have heard about the murder.

He must have tripped some sort of sensor when he went into the building. They'd sent two men in with the hope of shooting him, but had been prepared to blow themselves up if need be. At least, Shirazi had been prepared to do that. It was possible that his comrade hadn't been aware of the full extent of the plan. He hadn't seemed to know for sure that Jeremiah was there whereas Shirazi had seemed to know. Shirazi had a switch that could control both bombs. It was also likely rigged so that if his heart stopped they would explode.

He'd started running a second before Shirazi could detonate the bombs. It hadn't been enough to escape the blast, though. Twisted, broken metal had fallen on his hand after he hit the floor, taking the ring and middle fingers of his left hand at the knuckle. There were burns and lacerations all over his back and legs. Some of it was incredibly painful. In other parts the nerve endings had been seared and he couldn't feel anything.

The lack of feeling had made it that much more important that he could use the mirrors in the bathroom to inspect his back and make sure he wasn't bleeding without knowing it. He couldn't risk dying that way.

He sat on the floor of the bathroom panting, trying to get up the strength to leave. There were five more men out there who wanted him dead and they wouldn't stop until they were sure that it had happened. As soon as the firemen cleared out they'd be making their own inspection looking for bodies. Given that both their men had been ground zero for such a strong blast it was unlikely that they'd find anything left of them. And finding Jeremiah's severed fingers wouldn't be enough to satisfy them. They'd keep searching until they were sure.

If he was them this church would be the first place he'd look. That was why he had to move even if he didn't have the strength to. More than that, though, he had to think. It did no good to move if he just moved into another trap. They'd had a year to plan how they were going to take him down. Why go to such lengths he didn't know. They could have taken him out with a sniper rifle any time he showed up at the synagogue.

They want me to know who they are. They want to see my face and have me see theirs.

It was the only thing that made sense. This vendetta for them was more than operatives hunting down someone from the other side. This was deeply personal for them. It was rapidly becoming personal for him as well.

He was so grateful that Martin had agreed to put everyone into protective custody. He couldn't bear the thought of Cindy or any of the others being used as bait or ending up as collateral damage.

The only thing he knew about the others was that at least one of them would be there shortly to inspect the site. He had to be ready when they came. He needed to have the upper hand.

Using his good hand and holding onto a sink he hauled himself to his feet. The staff of the church would have a heck of a mess to clean up when they got back to work. There was blood all over the bathroom at this point. There was nothing he could do about it. He promised himself that if he made it through alive he'd give the church a small donation. They deserved it for providing sanctuary in his time of greatest need.

He made it out of the bathroom, struggling with wooziness as he did so. He needed to find a good vantage point to spy on whoever came to see their handiwork. He needed a place they wouldn't be likely to search, too.

The hotel across the street would be ideal, but he didn't think he'd be able to make it to a good spot without raising some alarms. He couldn't just check in given the shape he was in. As soon as anyone spotted him they'd see blood and they'd call the police.

He made it outside and his eyes fell on a car that was parked halfway up the block, the trunk facing toward the ruins of the check cashing building. There was some debris that had fallen on top of it. He'd noticed it earlier as well. Given its location he suspected that it might have belonged to the teller who had been killed in the store.

He walked as quickly as he could toward the car, trying to keep himself conscious and walking a straight line. Once at the car he tried the doors but discovered that they were locked. He cursed silently since he couldn't pick the lock without the use of both hands. He went around to the back and slid his hand underneath the car. Finally, his fingers brushed against a small box.

Relief surged through him as he pulled the box from its hiding place. It had attached to the car through use of a magnet and inside was a spare key. Jeremiah offered up a prayer of thanksgiving for G-d's provision as he used the key to get into the trunk.

Fortunately, the trunk was mostly empty. There was an emergency kit, jumper cables, and a pack of bottled water back there.

He crawled in and was able to lower it enough that it would appear closed at a glance, but he still had a slit to look through. He was able to open one of the water bottles and he drank as much as he dared. He couldn't risk dehydration on top of everything else.

The pain in his collarbone and hand was so intense that he wanted to scream. The burned skin that still had feeling chafed at the tightness of the quarters and he could feel the air around him heating up which made things even more unbearable.

He'd already taken painkillers from the church's first aid kit and he dared not take anymore. If he did this right he could use the pain to his advantage. Just enough pain kept him conscious and alert. Too much pain would knock him out or render him delirious. It was a delicate balance. Fortunately, it was not the first time he'd had to play this particular game with himself.

Now he just had to wait. And stay alive while he did so. He tried to focus on the terrorists, thinking about what their next moves would be. He was having a hard time concentrating, though, and he felt himself starting to drift. He shifted slightly allowing the friction against his burned skin to spike his pain levels slightly.

Cindy's face came to mind and he fixated on that instead. He had to get through this for her sake. He imagined their wedding day and what it would be like. She would make a gorgeous bride. He'd had a sneak peek of that at Joseph and Geanie's wedding. He would have known it was true even if he hadn't.

He wondered what dress she would get, what the design would be. She looked great in anything she wore but he found himself hoping that the neckline was low and not high. He could see her in something with short sleeves revealing her beautiful arms.

In his imagination she was wearing her hair up with some flowers in it. Her lips were red as roses and her eyes danced like they did when she was laughing and happy.

It was good to think of the future, of all the reasons why he had to make it out of this mess. He needed to protect her, and their life together. He couldn't let anyone take that away from them. Not terrorists or spy organizations or pastors or family members.

He was starting to drift again, and he was just about to shift positions when he heard the sound of a car approaching. It was slowing down. Moments later it stopped several feet away. He watched as four Iranian men got out of the car.

He'd found them.

And then, as one turned his head sharply toward Jeremiah's hiding place he realized in horror that they'd found him.

13

As the agents had rushed in to halt the fighting among the others, Cindy had seen her chance and she'd slipped out of the door and ran down the corridor. She made it to the parking garage and ran toward an exit. Her heart was pounding, and her broken arm jostled painfully, shooting fire through her with every step. She wouldn't stop or slow down, though. She couldn't.

Jeremiah needs me.

She had no idea where he was, but somehow she would find him.

The parking garage which hadn't looked that big the night before seemed to take forever to run across. With every step she expected to hear shouting. She figured she only had a few seconds before they realized she had escaped. She was almost to an exit when she heard the sound of a car approaching. She jumped behind a pillar just as a car pulled into the garage.

She moved slowly around the pillar, trying to keep it between her and the car. Finally, she was on the side closest to the exit. As soon as she left the safety of the pillar she risked being seen in the rearview mirror. Of course, she couldn't stay there forever because any second the guards would come running with the news that she had escaped.

She was about twenty-five feet away from the street. She took a deep breath, pushed off the pillar, and ran without looking back. She kept expecting to hear something, waited for the car to come zooming after her or to hear footsteps and shouting.

As soon as she was out of the structure she turned to her right. She ran up to the corner and took another right, trying to keep the building between her and her pursuers as long as she could. Once she was halfway down the block she ran across the street, praying that she could make it out of sight before they rounded the corner. When she made it to the next intersection, she turned left and dashed up a couple of yards.

There was a small hedge of bushes surrounding a tree which offered some shelter. She crouched down behind them as she struggled to catch her breath. Her heart was pounding so hard it felt like it was going to explode, and she felt like she couldn't get enough air. She couldn't remember ever having felt so bad after a run in her entire life. She started to feel light-headed and she realized she was gulping the air instead of just breathing.

Don't hyperventilate, she begged herself. That was the last thing she needed. If she passed out they would catch her and there would be no second chances at escape. She was very sure about that.

Just breathe. Don't pass out.

It felt like she was going to. She was angry at herself for being out of shape.

Serious gym time for me if I get out of this, she vowed.

Of course, she was injured and running on empty. She hadn't had any sleep and the few mouthfuls of Froot Loops she'd managed to get down hadn't been enough to fuel her up.

She kept straining her eyes and ears, trying to catch signs of pursuit. Of course, the way the blood was pounding in her ears she didn't have a shot at hearing pursuers coming after her.

God, please protect me, hide me, she prayed.

Her throat was dry, and it felt like the air was just hurting it more. Finally, though, her heart and breathing began to slow and she felt less light-headed. Her arm was throbbing uncontrollably, but there was nothing she could do about it at the moment.

She'd been lucky when Traci started the fight. She had barely heard what the other woman was screaming, but Cindy had seen when the two agents came through the door and she knew she'd never have a better chance at escape. She'd hoped that there weren't other agents in the hall and she'd been right. It would have only taken seconds, though, for them to realize she was gone.

Suddenly she heard a sound. She tried to still herself as best as she could, shrinking down even lower behind the bushes. She heard running footsteps. They were getting closer. Then, just when she thought she was about to be discovered, the footsteps stopped.

"Negative, I don't see her," a man said, voice calm and clear. "I don't know which way she went."

He couldn't have been more than half a dozen feet away. She wished more than anything she could hold her breath so that it wouldn't betray her, but she was struggling to get oxygen as it was.

"She'll never make it on foot."

Make it where? Where did they think she was heading? A moment later she realized they must be referencing where she was in relation to where Jeremiah was. Or, at least, where he had last been seen.

"Understood. I'm heading back now," the man said, frustration clear in his voice.

Getting outwitted by a civilian clearly didn't sit well with him, which made Cindy smile a little.

After a few moments she heard the footsteps retreat. Once she could no longer hear them she began to relax. She moved farther away from the building, making a few turns as she tried to get as much distance between her and her captors. She figured if she wound through the streets it would make it harder for them to find her than if she just picked a street and kept moving down it.

She finally began to breathe a little easier and the tightness in her chest loosened. She was reasonably certain that she was safe for the moment. Now it was time to get out of there and go help the man she loved.

She suddenly realized that there was just one problem with that.

As she stood on a street corner and looked around her heart began to sink. She had no identification and no money of any sort. Even worse, absolutely nothing around her looked familiar. Before she could find Jeremiah, she had to figure out where she was.

~

Mark was holding Rachel, rocking her back and forth while Traci fed Ryan and the rest tried to deal with the fallout from the fight and Cindy escaping. He himself was still a bit shell shocked, but he was trying to just be as calm as he could for Rachel.

Kyle was lying down with a frozen bag of something or other on his eye. His mom was busy fussing over him and ignoring the rest of them which was fine by him. The one he felt most sorry for was Don who looked about as helpless as a man could be in that moment. His daughter was gone and there was nothing he could do for her. Plus, his wife and son were in their own little world and both angry at him for not taking their side.

Geanie was wound up and Joseph was doing his best to try and keep her calm. Joseph himself looked on edge, frazzled.

Mark turned and looked at his wife and son. Traci had a serene expression on her face that frightened him given the circumstances. Just minutes before she'd been ready to kill Kyle.

So much for her celebrity crush on him.

It was silly, but that thought actually made him smile. He thought of Traci's sister, the one always trying to impress people with stories of the famous people she'd met. Next time she brought up seeing Chuck Norris he'd wager her that Traci could take him in a fair fight. She didn't have style or training but she more than made up for it with raw ferocity.

He'd always known that she was a passionate person, even if she usually held herself in check. What he'd seen a few minutes before had shocked him, though.

We all deal with stress and grief in our own way, he reminded himself.

Truth was he was proud of her. He was also very, very grateful she'd taken her frustrations out on someone he didn't like. Once she was done with the babies he'd help her ice her hand just to make sure it didn't swell too much. He'd be surprised if she hadn't at least sprained her wrist.

He smiled down at Rachel who had settled down and was blinking at him sleepily. She'd been fed first and now she was thinking of taking another nap. That was fine by him. The grownups had unpleasant business to discuss.

"You doing okay, Hon?" he asked Traci softly.

She was humming to herself and she looked up at him, her face absolutely glowing. "Much better, thank you," she said.

"Maybe I should encourage you to hit people more often," he whispered.

"It did feel good," she admitted with a gentle smile.

He shook his head. "Have I told you today how much I love you?"

"No, I don't think so."

"I love you more than the stars in the heavens," he said.

She blushed and he could tell that she was pleased with his answer.

He walked over to Joseph and Geanie. Geanie had tears streaking down her cheeks. Unlike Traci she hadn't been able to have the cathartic experience of punching Kyle. In that moment he felt sorry for her.

"Hey, you want to hold her?" he asked.

Geanie nodded eagerly. He gently handed Rachel to her and Geanie held her close, looking down at her with a smile.

Thank you, Joseph mouthed to him and Mark nodded. He was happy to help in whatever way he could.

Right now, they all needed each other, probably more than they ever had before. He tried not to think about Cindy and Jeremiah out there by themselves. There wasn't anything he could do to help them. He could, however, help the people in that room.

He went and sat down next to Don. "How are you holding up?" he asked quietly.

"Better than could be expected," Don said bluntly. "You?"

"I don't honestly know. I'm pretty much on autopilot at the moment."

"I get that."

Don chuckled.

"What?" Mark asked.

"Your wife has a heck of a right hook."

Mark shook his head. "After all these years she still surprises me."

"That's a good thing."

"Sorry she punched your son."

"Don't be. He had it coming," Don said with a sigh. "And frankly I'd much rather see your wife hit him than see Cindy hit him."

"That makes sense. It's probably a good thing Cindy was a lot more focused on what was happening out there than what was happening in here."

"I just hope she's safe," Don said, worry creeping into his voice.

"She's smart and a lot tougher than most people give her credit for. Herself included."

"She was telling me about an incident involving darts."

Mark smiled. "Yes, that was one of her more impressive acts. Her accuracy was uncanny. Almost as good as Jeremiah's."

"You played a game of darts with him?" Don asked.

Mark snorted. "More like tried to distract him with a game of darts and got my butt kicked."

"What do you think of him?"

Mark hadn't been expecting the question. He took a deep breath. "He was... *is* the best man I know. He loves Cindy more than anything. He's loyal, intense, and not someone I'd ever want to cross. But I love him like a brother. I trust him. And right now, I'm very, very scared for him."

"He has a lot of very loyal friends here. That's unusual for a man like him."

"What can I say? He's an unusual guy."

"Clearly."

"Look, I know it wasn't easy for him, learning to let people in, to make friends and build a community. I know it's still not always easy. He always thinks he has to protect people."

"Which is why we're all here," Don said, indicating the room.

"Yeah, exactly. I mean, I get it. I'm a cop. I work really hard to protect people that I care about, too. And sometimes I'm overzealous about it and sometimes I'm terrible at sharing how I'm feeling and asking for help."

Don smiled. "From where I'm sitting, you're doing just fine."

"Thanks for that, I appreciate it. The truth is that for a while I thought Jeremiah was going to freak out and disappear. Then one day, I stopped worrying about that."

"What day was that?" Don asked.

"Honestly? The day he stopped being a coward and asked Cindy to marry him. That's when I knew he was staying forever."

"Forever," Don echoed.

"Yeah," Mark said, feeling tears beginning to sting his eyes.

The two sat in silence for a moment and Mark knew they were both thinking about, both worrying about the same thing.

"He's a real resourceful guy," Mark said, his voice cracking. "He's made it out of a lot of really impossible situations."

Don nodded. "I'm sure he has. And he's got a lot to live for."

"Dang straight. Why, any moment he's going to come waltzing in having vanquished all his foes. And he'll give me holy hell for letting Cindy escape. And nothing I say will make a bit of difference. I can hear him lecturing me right now."

Don smiled. "No one *let* her escape."

"He wouldn't see it that way," Mark said. "But that's fine," he said, wiping at his eyes. His voice was starting to shake more, and he couldn't control it. He finally stopped trying to. "I want him to come in here and yell at me, just chew me out like there's no tomorrow and call me all kinds of names."

"Because then he'd be alive," Don said softly.

Mark nodded. "Then he'd be alive."

14

Cindy still had no idea where she was. None of the street names were even remotely familiar and she was starting to wonder if she was even still in Pine Springs. She honestly didn't know how long the car ride from Joseph's house to the underground bunker was. She was in an area that was mostly warehouses, and she didn't see any place where she could ask to use a phone.

She finally found a payphone and snatched the receiver off the hook. Then she hesitated. She'd been about to call the church and see if she could get hold of Dave or someone else. She had no idea what story Martin had told her coworkers about her, Geanie, and Joseph's absence, though, and didn't relish having to dodge the real explanation. The same thing went for Liam. Even though he knew some of Jeremiah's past, he was the man in charge of overseeing the current case against him. She couldn't risk bringing him into the loop. Not now.

Finally, she realized there was only one call she could make. Fortunately, her job had necessitated her making the call often enough that she had the number memorized. She called the synagogue.

She listened in agony as Marie picked up the phone and a recorded voice asked her if she would accept a collect call from Cindy Preston. She practically sobbed in relief when Marie said "yes" and they were connected.

"Cindy? What's wrong," Marie asked, smart enough to know Cindy wouldn't be calling the synagogue collect if it wasn't an emergency.

"I'm so sorry, but I have a huge favor to ask. I need you to pick me up."

"Okay. Where are you?"

"That's just it. I have no idea. I'm at the corner of Chestnut Street and Evergreen Place."

"Those names aren't familiar."

"To me either, but they have to be somewhere in or near Pine Springs. Maybe if you just look it up in a map program it will show you."

"I'll try."

"Thank you. And please hurry. It's a matter of life and death."

Marie hung up the phone so fast she didn't even say goodbye. Slowly Cindy put the receiver back. She turned and wrapped her arms around herself, praying that Marie would find her before anyone else did.

~

Jeremiah felt like a trapped animal, but he readied himself to act as the Iranian man approached the car. One of the other men shouted something that he couldn't quite make out. Everyone laughed and the man who was approaching the car stopped, turned and shouted something back.

The other three walked toward him, gesturing to the rubble. He strained to hear what they were saying. He finally started to make out the words and his mind quickly translated.

A shame about Ashkan.

Don't worry about him. He is with Allah now.

He was always too rash.

Yes, but thank Allah he took that weakling with him. He was a liability. I never understood why Ashkan recruited him.

Once the fire starts burning, the damp and the dry will burn together.

At least the devil of death is dead.

He can no longer interfere in our business here.

Or take more of our brothers.

He would have done well to kill all instead of just one.

It is not a mistake we would make.

Which is why we will kill his friends. We will not give them the opportunity to seek revenge later.

They have disappeared.

They will return once it is known that he is dead. We can kill them while they waste their tears for him.

We should search the area.

No need. Ashkan triggered the bomb on purpose. He killed the devil as he swore to do. No one could have survived that blast.

But we should be thorough.

We do not have time. We need to finish the transaction tonight before too many people ask questions about what happened here.

Agreed.

You all know what you need to do. Hazim, you take the dead man's car and pick up our brother. We will meet in four hours at the hotel.

The three men turned back to the car they'd arrived in and Hazim, who was closest to him, pulled keys out of his pocket.

Jeremiah tensed, hoping the man wouldn't open the trunk. To his relief Hazim walked past the back of the car. Seconds later he could feel Hazim climb into the front seat as the car settled slightly.

He gritted his teeth. Riding in the trunk of a car was never ideal even under the best of circumstances. Life was about to get even harder really quick.

He could see the other car drive away. Even so, he dared not do anything. He didn't know where the fifth man was, and he didn't know where they were all supposed to be meeting. If he hoped for any shot at getting all of them he needed to ride this out. No matter what it cost him.

~

Mark was sitting at the table staring down a C.I.A. agent and he didn't like it any more than Martin did.

"Where is she heading?" Martin asked.

"To help Jeremiah."

"And where exactly is she going to do that?"

"I wish I knew, but you never told us where he was or where you found… what you found. I don't know where he is or where she thinks he is. I just know there was no way you were going to hold her while he was out there injured."

"She is stubborn, I'll give her that," Martin said with a sigh.

For a moment Mark almost felt sorry for the guy. He'd had to put people in protective custody before, and he knew how frustrating it was when someone just kept refusing to let you protect them.

"Look, you've got access I'm sure to all the cameras in the county. Between traffic cameras, security cameras, ATM cameras, I'm sure it wouldn't be too hard for you to find her," Mark said.

Martin shook his head. "I can't pull manpower to do that."

There was a tension in him that had to go beyond his frustration over losing Cindy. Mark leaned forward, examining the other man closely.

"You're running some kind of operation locally."

"Of course we're not." Martin said. "We're not the F.B.I. after all."

"Yeah, I know you're not supposed to operate on U.S. soil, but I believe there are exceptions when it comes to certain areas. Terrorism for instance."

"You suspect someone of terrorism call the N.S.A.," Martin said. "I'm just here to babysit."

Mark shook his head and gestured around the room. "This goes beyond just helping out a colleague in a time of crisis. The terrorists who are after Jeremiah – there's another reason they're here, isn't there?"

"You know with that suspicious and paranoid mind of yours, I'm surprised you're not working for us."

Mark held up his hands. "Not for me. My wife likes me home for dinner every night. Even if it is late some nights."

"Most nights, I'm guessing. You seem pretty dedicated to your work."

"You aren't going to tell me anything, are you?" Mark asked in frustration.

"No, but eventually you'll tell me something."

"Why would I do that?"

"Because you want to protect Cindy even more than I do. Look, there's a reason I'm talking to you first. As a law enforcement officer, you understand that it's just too dangerous to have her running around out there. It's dangerous for her, dangerous for everyone here, and dangerous for Jeremiah."

He wasn't wrong and Mark's sense of loyalty and faith in his friends was being put at odds with every instinct he had as a cop.

"You're too smart for your own good," Mark growled.

"I'm as smart as my country needs me to be," Martin countered. "Look, every second we lose at this point is crucial."

Mark took a deep breath. "You think Jeremiah is dead."

"If we were talking about any other man it would be a foregone conclusion. But, I've seen him in action. He's one slippery son-of-a-gun when he has to be." Martin leaned forward and lowered his voice. "The fingers we found were severed clean."

"Not blown off?" Mark asked, also dropping his voice.

"Yes, more like cut by something sharp. In fact, they were intact enough that we've got them on ice."

"You mean, it would be possible to reattach them?"

Martin nodded. "But there's less than ten hours at this point before that's no longer even a possibility. If Jeremiah is alive he's going to be in rough shape and he's going to need a hospital soon or losing a couple of fingers will be the least of his worries."

~

Jeremiah blacked out twice from pain as he got bounced around in the trunk. He was on the verge of losing consciousness a third time when the car came to a halt and the engine turned off. He fought through the haze of pain, knowing he had to be ready at a second's notice if Hazim decided to open the trunk.

A far bigger threat at the moment, though, was that he was going to be sick. The motion of the car, the blood loss, and the pain were all combining to make his stomach churn. He couldn't risk it, especially not now with the car stopped. Hazim would hear him vomiting and kill him while he was helpless.

Sneezing, coughing, and vomiting. They were the three deadly autonomic functions. Any one of them could get a man killed when he was trying to hide. He'd seen it before. He'd taken advantage of it before. He prayed that it wouldn't be his undoing now.

His desperation started to grow, and he realized his only chance might be to act before his body betrayed him. He had a hand on the emergency release handle for the trunk. In his current physical condition he didn't like his odds. He'd give himself one chance in five to come out on top. The only thing he had in his favor was the element of surprise. Unfortunately, he couldn't move fast enough to really take advantage of that.

He heard footsteps retreating and he closed his eyes and prayed as hard as he could. Finally, the sickness began to ease up. Once it did, he set to work trying to figure out his best course of action. If he took out Hazim and the man he was picking up now then he would only have three left to deal with. The only problem was all he knew about the location of the others was that they were going to be at a hotel. Unless one of the men had some clue on them as to where that was then he'd be in trouble.

It was possible there was information on their phone or credit card receipts in their pocket that he could use to try and deduce the information. Of course, if they were being smart they weren't leaving things like that to chance. He wouldn't in their shoes.

The car they had just stolen from a dead man; so there was no hope of finding any kind of rental agreement or ownership documentation in it that could even give him a last name to work with.

There were probably half a dozen hotels in Pine Springs and literally hundreds in a thirty-mile radius. He could start randomly calling them asking if anyone with the last name Shirazi had been there, but the hotel staff might only have the last name of whichever man had rented the room or rooms. It was also possible that they were using assumed names. He would have assumed that Shirazi was an assumed name, but the other men had called him that with no one around to hear them. Still, he was certain they had wanted him to find the connection at the check cashing place so they could trap him. At any rate, by randomly calling hotels and blindly taking stabs in the dark he risked alerting the terrorists that someone was looking for them.

Times like this were when one needed to marshal their resources. Which, in his case, was just him. Normally he would have been confident that was enough, but his injuries were extensive. Truth be told, right now the only thing whatsoever that he had going for him was the fact that they thought he was already dead.

Wait! That's not true, he realized.

They also had a business deal that evening to distract them. It meant that they would likely be hyper alert and vigilant, but they would be paying attention mostly to the other parties involved.

Given the likely nature of that business deal it might be a good idea to call in Martin. In fact, it was possible Martin already had an inkling about it. Although he was reasonably certain that Martin didn't know where the men were staying. Otherwise he would have expected the man to share it with him. It certainly would have made things a lot easier.

He had a burner phone with him. He could make the call, but then he'd have to toss the phone, particularly if there was any chance of Martin trying to stop him or Cindy or Mark trying to coerce Martin into tracking him. He had no doubts they'd already tried to beg and bully information out of the man. Martin was tough, though. He could handle it. If Jeremiah hadn't thought he could he wouldn't have entrusted him with his loved ones in the first place.

He tensed suddenly as he heard two sets of footsteps approaching. He waited, hoping that they wouldn't come near the trunk. His best bet was to wait until they arrived at the hotel and then work out a plan based on the situation he found there. He just hoped it wouldn't be a long drive.

He could hear the two men talking low, and strained to make out what they were saying. It was casual conversation, the weather, a girl one of them had seen that was pretty. A car door opened, and Jeremiah started to relax.

Then in a clear voice the second man said, "Open the trunk."

15

Cindy finally spotted Marie's car. She waved
frantically, and the other woman pulled over in front of her.
Cindy got into the passenger seat as quickly as she could.

"Get us out of here," she begged.

Marie hit the gas and the car rocketed forward.

"How on earth did you get out here?" Marie asked. "No,
wait. Don't tell me. You said it was a matter of life and
death. Where do you need me to take you?"

Cindy had been thinking about that since she hung up
the phone and she still didn't have a good answer.

"I don't know," she admitted.

"Okay, that makes my job significantly more difficult,"
Marie said.

"I know. I'm sorry."

"Well, I'll start driving back toward the synagogue and
when you figure it out let me know."

"Thank you," Cindy said.

She sat in the passenger seat and wracked her brain, but
realized she had no clue where to even start looking for
Jeremiah. After about fifteen minutes she realized that
there was only one place she could look for help and she
felt foolish for not having asked sooner. She closed her
eyes.

God, please help me find Jeremiah, she prayed silently.
Please, let him be okay and let me be a help to him. God, I

*have nowhere to look and a terrible feeling that time is
running out. Please, please give me a sign.*

She opened her eyes and took a deep breath. She looked
around and realized that she was finally in more familiar
territory. She forced herself to take deep, even breaths and
tried to listen to see if God was trying to tell her something.
She didn't hear anything, though. There was no quiet
prompting, no place suddenly popped into her mind. She
kept breathing and praying. She struggled not to let her fear
and desperation overwhelm her.

God is good. God will help me, she kept repeating to
herself.

*God, I know you brought Jeremiah and I together. You
have to help us now*, she begged.

"Any ideas yet?" Marie asked, interrupting her prayers.

"No," Cindy said, struggling to keep the frustration out
of her voice. "I keep praying that God will send me a sign,
but so far there's been nothing."

"You really think you will get something obvious?"
Marie asked.

"Yes, absolutely. He has to help me. I need to know
where to go," Cindy said. "It's too important."

She heard a siren and suddenly a police car flew past on
the other side of the street. It was followed moments later
by a second one.

"That's the sign!" she shouted, causing Marie to jump
and almost lose control of the car.

"What?"

"The police cars! Follow them!"

"I'm not sure-"

"Do it!"

Marie hung a sudden U-turn in the middle of the road. "You're paying for it if I get a ticket," she warned.

"I'd pay a hundred tickets, just follow them," Cindy begged.

"Okay, hold on," Marie said as she floored it.

The car leapt forward and in moments they were tearing down the road. The police cars came into sight ahead and Marie wove in and out of the cars between her and them. She was muttering to herself the entire time, but Cindy didn't care. She kept her eyes glued on the police cars. There were two of them. The only reason two of them were going somewhere had to be something big. And she believed deep in her heart that it wasn't a car accident or anything like that.

She believed they were leading her to Jeremiah.

~

Martin was thorough, Mark would give him that. After talking to him he began talking to Joseph.

"You've offered sanctuary to Cindy many times."

"That's what friends are for," Joseph said calmly.

"Where do you think she'd go now?"

"Where do you think she'd go?" Joseph countered.

"I don't know, that's why I'm asking you."

"It seems to me that you have far more skills when it comes to predicting behavior than I do. You also have more resources than I currently have."

"I have more resources than you ever have," Martin said calmly.

Joseph raised an eyebrow. "I wouldn't be so certain about that."

Martin smirked at him. "All your money still doesn't put you on an even footing with the U.S. government."

"I agree. I have a leg up. I'm not bound by all the same rules that the government is," Joseph said.

"Look, I want to find Cindy and keep her safe," Martin said.

"So do I," Joseph said.

"So, help me do that," Martin urged.

Joseph leaned forward. "I'll make you a deal."

"What's that?" Martin asked.

"You come work for me at three times your current salary. I can always use someone of your skills. Better pay, better hours, more benefits. Then, we can all get out of here together and find our friends and bring them home."

Despite himself Mark felt his mouth gaping open. Every once in a while Joseph exhibited so much moxie that it was shocking. Now he was seeing Joseph the businessman, the negotiator. Just because Joseph spent most of his time laid back and letting others taking care of his business affairs clearly didn't mean he couldn't hold his own with the best of them.

Martin stared at him for a long minute and then chuckled. He leaned back and folded his hands in his lap.

"It's an intriguing offer, but I'll have to pass."

"Make me a counter-offer. I'm sure we can come to a mutually beneficial arrangement," Joseph said. "A nicer house for your family, exotic vacations, the best colleges for your kids."

"Our house is plenty nice, I've had my fill of exotic locales, and my kids are smart enough they'll get full rides wherever they want to go. Besides, there's one thing that you can't offer me that my current job does."

"And what exactly is that?" Joseph asked.

"The opportunity to serve my country. Protecting a dozen people is not nearly as stimulating as protecting three hundred and twenty-seven million people."

Joseph actually laughed. "I wouldn't be so certain of that if I were you. You should see the kind of trouble the right dozen people can get into."

"I'm starting to get an inkling."

Mark was doing his best not to laugh out loud. The whole conversation was fascinating to watch. It was also a bit ludicrous, but then he would have been disappointed at anything less.

Martin finally dismissed Joseph with a wave of his hand. Geanie went and took her husband's place and Martin looked her over. Mark got comfortable, eager to see how this particular interview would go.

~

Cindy's heart was in her throat the entire time that they were chasing after the police cars. She didn't know where Marie had learned to drive but the other woman was frighteningly good at it. At least, that's what Cindy kept telling herself. Because otherwise, Marie was just frightening, and Cindy didn't want to deal with that. She kept telling herself that they weren't going to die in some horribly fiery crash because the other woman had skills.

The police cars turned right, and Marie slid into the turn practically on their heels. Cindy wanted to suggest that they not ride right on the second car's bumper, but didn't want to break whatever concentration Marie had. There was absolutely nothing subtle about the way she was driving, and they were one hundred percent certain to get at least a half dozen tickets by the time they all got to where they were going. Speeding, the illegal U-turn, and reckless driving were topping the list so far.

All three cars blew through a stop sign and Cindy added it to the mental tally. That was fine, because in the end she was going to find Jeremiah and that was all that mattered.

They made a left turn and she cringed as she heard Marie's tires screaming as she skidded through the intersection. Cindy had her hands braced on the dashboard.

God, don't let us die, she prayed.

Suddenly the two cars in front of them slowed and Marie nearly rear-ended the one in front of her. She managed to hit the brakes just in time. Up ahead there was a small knot of people clustered on a sidewalk in front of what looked like an office building. They were near a car that had its trunk open.

The police cars pulled to a stop. Marie stopped behind them and Cindy jumped out of the car and ran forward. A second later she saw the body on the ground.

~

Mark watched Martin question the others with varying results. His darling wife, Traci, was certainly the most uncooperative of the group. She refused to say anything. She just sat and glared daggers at the man. From Mark's perspective it was actually pretty funny. She had clearly had it with the whole situation. He couldn't blame her.

When Martin finally gave up Traci came over to him. Mark smiled at her and chuckled.

"It's not funny," she said glaring at him.

"Whoa, honey, I'm on your side," he said. "You're still pretty riled up from hitting Kyle. I enjoyed watching that, by the way."

"If he's smart he and his mother will keep their mouths shut," she growled.

He put a hand on her shoulder and she jumped.

"Not that I'm not enjoying your hostility toward them, because I am, very much, but I think there's something else wrong."

Traci looked up at him and as always he was overwhelmed by her beauty and how much he loved her. He slid an arm around her waist.

"What's wrong?" he asked.

"What do you think?" she snapped.

He sighed. "I know what's wrong-wrong, but your reactions seem a bit more intense than the rest of us."

She looked like she was about to say something snarky, but she stopped herself. A shudder passed over her and she leaned into him slightly.

"I'm claustrophobic," she whispered.

He frowned. He had never known her to be. "Since when?" he asked.

She bit her lip and looked away. He put a finger under her chin and tilted her face back to his.

"Since I was kidnapped by those horrible men," she admitted.

He blinked in surprise. The men who had killed the homeless and kidnapped their dogs years ago had also kidnapped Traci.

"Why didn't you tell me?" he asked.

She shrugged. "I thought it would pass. Then, when you had the trouble at work, I didn't want to put more stress on you. I've been dealing with it. It's almost never an issue, but here-"

"There's no windows and people are stopping you from leaving the room," he said, realization dawning on him.

She nodded. "At first it wasn't bad. We were all here, I was trying to make a game of it, like a big slumber party."

"But then you heard the news about Jeremiah and Cindy escaped and you were still stuck?"

She nodded. "It's feeling a lot less like a slumber party and more like a wake."

He wrapped his arms around her and hugged her. He realized a second later that if she was feeling claustrophobic that might not be the best move. He loosened his grip, but she wrapped herself around him, clinging hard.

"I'm so sorry. I had no idea," he told her.

"It's okay. It's stupid, I know," she muttered against his shoulder.

"It's not stupid. Not all scars leave marks on the body. It doesn't make them any less real," he said.

She clung to him harder and he stroked her hair.

"Thank you," she said.

"Thank you for telling me what was wrong."

He wished he'd known sooner. He could beat himself up all day for not having noticed or for not being available when she needed to talk, but at this point that wouldn't do either of them any good.

"Do you... want to pray about it?" he asked, scarcely believing what he was suggesting.

She nodded.

"Okay. I'll get Geanie and Joseph."

She shook her head.

"But they're the ones who know what to do, what to say."

"I need to hear it from you."

"Oh. Okay," he said, feeling completely inadequate to the task. "Um, hey, God, please, uh, help Traci stop feeling claustrophobic. And help us to get out of here. And let Jeremiah be alive."

"Amen," Traci said.

He couldn't help but wonder what was wrong with him that he had started praying. He soon decided that there was time enough to figure that out later. At the moment he really needed to get her out of there.

"Hey, Martin!" he called.

The agent turned away from Carol with a frown. Mark nodded, and the man walked over.

"What is it?" he asked.

"We need to get her out of here. She's claustrophobic," Mark said.

"Ah, I see," Martin said. "I can walk her outside for a few minutes, but that's all I can do."

"That's not going to cut it," Mark said.

"I'm telling you my hands are tied."

"And I'm telling you-"

Martin's phone rang, and he pulled it out of his jacket and turned away. He started walking toward the door.

"This is Martin."

He was opening the door when Mark heard him ask, "Jeremiah, is that you?"

146

16

Mark let go of Traci and lunged forward. He grabbed Martin by the shoulder before the man could exit the room and yanked him back hard. Martin spun, his free hand moving lightning fast. His fingers wrapped around Mark's throat and squeezed.

Mark jerked back, but the agent held on and shook his head at him. His eyes looked like cold steel and Mark realized the depth of his mistake. He had assumed that Martin was an analyst or a paper-pusher. He had a very mild, non-threatening demeanor. But at that moment Mark realized he was dealing with a field agent, a man trained to kill who would do so if pushed.

"I'm having some difficulty impressing upon your friends the importance of them staying put," Martin said, squeezing hard enough to cut off Mark's air.

Mark's instincts told him to fight back, to grab at the man's hand even though his grip was incredibly strong. Fortunately, he was able to override that response and instead he raised his hands in surrender.

Martin held him for a moment longer, letting him know with a look that he was most definitely the one in charge and that he would not be so tolerant in the future. Then he let go and Mark staggered back. He felt Traci grab hold of him as he rubbed his throat. There were going to be bruises for sure.

Martin refocused all his attention on the phone call. "Where?" he asked sharply. After a moment he said, "You're going to need help. Let us assist you." There was another pause before Martin continued. "You're injured. You need a hospital."

It was clear to Mark that the conversation was not going Martin's way. He watched the muscles in the agent's jaw clench.

"You should know that Cindy is in the wind... Yeah, yeah, kill me later, but right now we both have problems."

Everyone in the room had come up behind Mark, eager to hear the news. Martin scowled at all of them, but no one moved.

"You should know that we found... your missing fingers. I've got them on ice... Yeah, thank me if we get through this. The clock is ticking you know... I swear, you're going to be the death of me. Fine, I'll see what I can do."

Martin hung up and faced the rest of them. "Yes, he's alive. Yes, he's in critical condition. No, he's not going to stop. I've got to go."

Martin turned back to the door.

Mark took a step forward.

Without even looking at him Martin lowered his voice and growled. "Not now."

Mark believed the threat in his voice and he stepped back. Martin headed out the door, closing it behind him.

Everyone began talking at once until Mark finally turned around to address them. "I don't think we're getting out of here until whatever is happening out there is over. So, what we need to focus on is handling Jeremiah's legal difficulties so we can sort that out before he gets back."

"Agreed," Don said. "Let's think about what we know."

"Good," Mark said, heading toward the table.

Geanie, Joseph, Don, and Traci moved quickly to join him. Kyle and Carol again retreated to their own corner of the room where they talked quietly. It was just as well. Mark knew Traci wouldn't be able to let it go if the two started being idiots again. He doubted that any of them would be able to let it go at this point.

"Alright, he's been accused of four murders," Mark said. "Let's start with the easiest one. The dead guy who showed up on Jeremiah's lawn."

"What do we know about him?" Don asked.

"He was a former spy turned homeless guy. He was going by the name of Peter at the time of his death. He seems to have been killed because he witnessed terrorists killing an Iranian student."

"Then how are they even accusing Jeremiah of this?" Don asked with a frown.

"Keenan's on a witch hunt, pure and simple. I just don't know why."

"Do you have proof that the terrorists killed the man?" Traci asked. "As I recall I was in the hospital giving birth during that whole investigation."

"You were," Mark said, picking up his wife's hand and kissing it. "I have proof that Asim, the student who was killed by his brothers, gave a letter to Peter to mail to his girlfriend if something happened to him. Everything else was pretty clear, but nothing I could actually show Keenan on paper. Plus, it all ended up running into the terrorist thing Jeremiah and Cindy dealt with in Israel, so…" He shrugged.

"So, it seems like our friendly neighborhood C.I.A. agent might have something to say about the matter," Don said.

"Heh. Not as friendly as he looks, trust me," Mark said touching his throat. "Plus, I'm not sure how willing he'd be to go on record with my department."

"I'm sure he has a way he could help," Don said.

"It's worth a try," Geanie said.

"You're right," Mark said. "The man was definitely killed because of his closeness to Azim, who Jeremiah never even met."

"Great, one down, let's keep going. Number two," Joseph said.

"Number two is a lot trickier. It's the terrorist at your guys' wedding, the one who was trying to kill Cindy," Mark said.

"What's so tricky about that one?" Don asked.

Mark cast a glance toward Kyle and Carol, but they were engaged in a conversation of their own and clearly not paying attention. He lowered his voice anyway, just to be on the safe side. "The problem is, Jeremiah actually did kill him."

"Oh," Geanie said, clearly startled.

"Who would know that?" Don asked, brow furrowing.

"Only me," Mark said. "I caught him right after. He gave me a line about the woman who was going after Joseph being responsible. And she's insane, so her answers about anything are immediately suspect. But, he told me later. The man was a terrorist, somehow related to the ones he's dealing with now."

"So, if it's a terrorist, that also seems like something we can pull Martin in on," Don said. "I mean, someone's going to have to clean up the aftermath of whatever is going on out there," he said, waving his hand to the outside world. "I say this gets packaged with that, whatever the explanation is."

"And I can swear that Jeremiah was never out of my sight," Geanie said defiantly, lifting her chin.

"That's perjury," Mark said.

"In all the chaos, the only ones who would know that are sitting at this table," she said.

"Yeah, he was with both of us during the chaos. He got us away from the front of the sanctuary and stayed with us until it was over," Joseph said.

"I'm not sure-" Mark began.

"There's nothing we said in the police reports that would contradict that. I'm quite sure of it," Geanie said. "We'll both swear that he was with us all along and couldn't be responsible for that man. He was another victim of psycho chick's machinations as far as I'm concerned. I'll tell Keenan as much."

"I still don't understand why Keenan was even looking into these murders," Traci said. "And why was he so quick to blame Jeremiah?"

"That brings us to the third problem," Mark said, taking a deep breath. "Keenan has somehow gotten it in his head that Jeremiah killed Not Paul."

"That's preposterous," Geanie said after a moment. "The assassins up at Green Pastures killed Paul when he went to rescue people."

"That case has been shut for a couple of years," Joseph said with a frown. "What on earth made him open it?"

"Here's where things get really weird," Mark said. "Someone came forward and claimed to witness it.

Whatever they said led Keenan to get a search warrant. He found a Barrett sniper rifle in Jeremiah's house. That's the same type of weapon that killed Not Paul."

Don looked at him in surprise. "That's a serious piece of weaponry, and not something that your average guy is going to have just lying around. Besides, Jeremiah wouldn't be stupid enough to keep a murder weapon."

"Agreed," Mark said.

"Two of the kids saw what happened, Noah and Sarah. Either of them could easily vouch for the fact that Jeremiah was right there and didn't have a weapon like that on him," Joseph said with a frown.

"How do you know?" Don asked.

"I read all the reports and statements since I was on the board that managed that property for several area churches and groups. So far of the three this is literally the most absurd and the most easily disproven. I don't understand," Joseph said. "I mean, Keenan is a detective and I'm assuming they don't just hand those badges out to idiots."

Mark nodded. "You're right. I've been so swept up in the stress and fear that I've been thinking about this all wrong. The only one they even have a shred of evidence for is that one and its patently wrong."

"So, I'm starting to really wonder who's framing Jeremiah? Is it a terrorist, someone else or maybe even Keenan?" Joseph asked.

"That's crazy," Mark said, not even wanting to think about it.

"Is it?" Traci broke in. "It's not like we haven't dealt with a corrupt cop from your department before. Heck, I was kidnapped by one," she said, her voice hardening at the end.

"But what could he possibly have against Jeremiah?" Joseph asked.

"Maybe not him personally, but someone else?" Geanie suggested.

"So, what about the fourth problem?" Don broke in.

"Ah, yes, the pastor at the church. Apparently he and Jeremiah have had some words and he gave Cindy crap for wanting to get married to Jeremiah," Mark said. "Other than that conflict, as far as I can tell he doesn't have anything else on the murder."

"Do we know who might have wanted the pastor dead?" Traci asked.

"Ben pissed off a lot of people when Cindy quit her job because of him. She's back, though, and I can't see any of those people doing more than yelling at him," Joseph said.

Geanie nodded in agreement.

"Cindy and I visited the crime scene," Don said, speaking up.

All eyes swiveled to him.

"And?" Joseph asked.

"We found one thing the cops had apparently missed. There was a torn-out page of his day planner. It was crumpled up under his desk. It showed that he had a meeting scheduled late night the night he was killed."

"With who?" Mark asked, leaning forward eagerly.

"It just had two initials. J.S.."

"That's not good," Mark muttered.

"Cindy was going to go over the church directory, see if there was anyone else with those initials since she couldn't think of anyone off the top of her head. She didn't get a chance," Don said grimly.

Mark frowned. "How on earth did the officers who went over the place miss that?"

"I don't know. We were only there for a couple of minutes and we found it easily enough. Perhaps too easy, if you know what I mean."

"Like it could have been planted there just like the rifle was planted in Jeremiah's house?" Traci asked.

"I'm just saying that if the pastor tore out the paper, he would have put it in a trash can. His place seemed pretty orderly. And if the killer tore out the paper they would have destroyed it or taken it with them."

"So, why didn't Keenan find it?" Mark wondered.

"Do you know if he was actually at the scene himself? Maybe if he left it he was hoping another cop would find it," Geanie suggested.

"That seems like a stretch."

Traci leaned toward Geanie and Joseph. "Is there anyone at the church with those initials?"

The two looked at each other.

"Well, I'm a J.C.," Joseph said. "Jordan's last name doesn't start with an S."

"Neither does Pastor Jake's or Jesse who heads the women's ministry," Geanie pointed out.

"Anyone else?" Mark asked.

"Grrr, I don't know! If we were in the office this would literally take me two minutes to figure out," Geanie said, the frustration strong in her voice.

He held up a hand. "We'll look when we can."

"That's assuming that the meeting was with someone from the church. Or that there even was a meeting and the whole thing wasn't just a red herring for our benefit. Or someone else's" Don said.

"Just how many enemies does Jeremiah have do you think?" Traci asked.

"The number is probably scary high," Mark said with a snort.

"Not just that, but people who would want to harm him in this way and not just kill him? I mean, I'm sure there's a line around the block of people that want to see him dead. But how many of those would want to see him in prison?"

"They could be trying to break him, strip away his network, his freedom, everything before killing him," Don offered.

Something was growing inside Mark's mind, though. He was beginning to think that they were going about this all the wrong way, looking in the wrong direction.

"What is it?" Traci asked him suddenly. "You've got that look on your face."

"Maybe we're asking the wrong question," he said.

"How do you mean?" Joseph asked.

"What if we shouldn't be trying to figure out who wants to hurt Jeremiah?"

"Well, clearly someone does. But, what are you thinking? What should we be trying to figure out?" Geanie asked.

Mark took a deep breath. There was a sudden sureness that was washing through him. He was on the right track and he knew it. He looked around at the others. "What if we should be trying to figure out who wants to hurt Cindy?"

17

"Ma'am, please move aside," a police officer said, pushing past Cindy.

All around police were filing out of cars. They started by pushing the crowd back away from the dead man on the ground. Another one began making a perimeter around the car and the body using yellow police tape.

Cindy moved forward, and another officer attempted to stop her.

"Please," she begged. "I think that might be my fiancé."

"Okay, don't touch anything," he said, compassion in his eyes.

Cindy moved forward, her feet feeling like lead. She didn't want to look, but she had to know the truth.

Finally, she was close enough to look down and get a good look.

Relief swept through her as she realized it wasn't Jeremiah. It looked like a middle eastern man. He had a look of surprise on his face and blood covering the front of his shirt.

Cindy turned away, shaking with relief.

"Was it him?" the policeman who had let her through asked.

She shook her head, "No. I've never seen that man before, and I'm so relieved," she burst out.

He nodded. "Good luck finding your fiancé."

"Thank you," she said.

She walked swiftly back to the car. "Thanks, I've got it from here," she told Marie.

"Are you sure?" the other woman asked, skepticism in her voice.

Cindy nodded firmly. "I'm positive. Thank you so much for all your help."

"You're welcome," Marie said. "If you don't need me I'm going to skedaddle before someone tries to write me up for all those tickets I earned."

"It's a good idea," Cindy agreed. "I will see you later."

Marie nodded before backing her car up and then slowly easing it around. Cindy watched until she was partway down the street then turned back to the crime scene. There was an alleyway between two buildings and she headed for it. If she was running from someone that's where she would have gone.

Once she was partway down it and sure no one was watching her she started looking around. Her heart skipped a beat when she saw drops of what looked like fresh blood on the ground.

She told herself that it was possible the blood wasn't his, but given what little she already knew about what he'd been through she was worried. Whoever's blood it was, though, she had to find Jeremiah fast before things got worse for him than they already were.

She sent up another prayer for Jeremiah's safety. Then she struck out down the alleyway, trying to determine how she was going to catch up with whoever she was following.

~

"Are you suggesting that someone killed Pastor Ben just so they could frame Jeremiah and get to Cindy?" Joseph asked.

Mark nodded.

"Isn't that a little extreme?" Joseph asked.

"More like a lot extreme," Geanie muttered.

"Is it really?" Traci asked.

"We've been fixating on his enemies. Maybe we should be looking at hers," Mark said.

Don frowned. "My daughter has enemies?"

"Um," Mark said, feeling suddenly awkward.

Traci put a hand on Don's arm. "Cindy has helped put many criminals behind bars. You can't do that without making some of them enemies."

"We still don't know for sure who hired the man to kill Leo in her house do we? That same killer tried to kill her on her way to the hospital," Geanie spoke up.

Don blanched. "One doesn't like hearing those kinds of things about their daughter," he said.

"I'm sorry," Traci said. "But, if it helps us put a stop to all this…"

"Then I'm in," he said.

"I swear that whole debacle over the secretary will just not go away," Mark said.

"Kind of like the whole debacle about Not Paul," Traci said pertly.

Mark rolled his eyes. "Point taken. At least Not Paul's ghost or someone who knew him isn't trying to kill me over it."

"Oh really? And how did you get stabbed by a banker then?" Traci demanded.

Mark touched his shoulder involuntarily. "That was more of a misunderstanding."

Traci snorted derisively, but let it go.

"I still don't understand how Keenan has gotten this bee in his bonnet, particularly since the case records should pretty clearly indicate that Jeremiah had nothing to do with either Peter or Paul's deaths," Don said.

"After Paul was killed I was temporarily, um, suspended," Mark said, really not wanting to go into all of that with the older man. "Our case work got split up and according to Keenan he ended up with a notebook or something where Paul had been keeping notes on his suspicions regarding Jeremiah. He thought Jeremiah had something to do with Peter's death and he died long before we knew otherwise. But apparently Paul laid out all his suspicions pretty intensely. Keenan has himself convinced that Jeremiah has a deep, dark secret that he killed Paul to keep," Mark explained.

"But Jeremiah does have a deep, dark secret," Don said with a frown.

"Yeah, but not one Paul knew or Keenan knows," Mark said.

"So, an old journal and possibly someone who helped frame Jeremiah. That's what we're looking at."

"That's about the size of it."

"I think you're onto something, though, Mark. If Keenan had these suspicions all this time, why wait to act on them? It's the Pastor's death that tipped him over the edge. That and whatever information he got that enabled him to get a warrant to search Jeremiah's house," Traci said.

"Thanks, Hon," Mark said, appreciating the support. "Look, I know Jeremiah made enemies, and I know that Keenan is sniffing around like a bloodhound that just won't let go, but I can't shake the feeling that there's a piece to this puzzle that we just keep missing."

"So, let's find it," Geanie said.

"There's nothing we can't figure out when we put our minds together," Traci said, her face and voice showing determination. "So, let's figure out who else Keenan might have been talking to. Someone who wants to hurt Cindy by destroying Jeremiah."

~

Jeremiah was literally running on empty. He had very little blood and no energy left. He knew he couldn't stop, though. His focus kept drifting which was a bad sign. Over and over again he kept talking to himself. Actually, in truth, he was imagining that he was talking to Cindy.

He had gotten lucky back at the car. Only the one man had been standing behind the car when the trunk was opened. He'd been able to shoot him in the heart and the man had died instantly.

Jeremiah had rolled out of the trunk just in time to see the other man jump out of the car and start to run. Jeremiah had shot, but only managed to get him in the arm as he turned down an alley.

Fortunately, he had left his cell phone behind in the car. It looked like he'd been in the middle of sending a text. Jeremiah had pocketed his phone and pursued. That pursuit was painfully slow, though, and his quarry was fast.

160

He couldn't stop. He couldn't risk the man being able to warn the others of what had happened. He did make a brief call to Martin letting him know about the weapons deal that was likely going down that night and inquiring if he knew what hotel the men were referencing. Martin had admitted that he did not know, but that they did have eyes on the seller. He tried to get Jeremiah to go to a hospital and let them handle it from there.

He couldn't risk something going wrong, though, and the men surviving. He needed them dead so there was no chance they'd tell anyone else who he was or where to find him.

Martin had also let him know that Cindy had escaped. He was furious, but not entirely surprised. She always surprised him with her resourcefulness. It made it that much more crucial that he find these guys before they could find her.

So, he kept walking, following the drops of blood left behind by Hazim. He knew he should be stalking his prey silently, but his feet were dragging as he shuffled along. And he had to keep muttering to keep himself focused, moving, and conscious. It was a terrible trade-off, but one that had to be made.

"I'm sorry to put you through all this, Cindy," he said, imagining her in his head. He pretended she was walking beside him. He could almost see her, hear her voice. It made him feel less alone.

He hesitated as he approached a corner, worried that Hazim could be just around it, waiting to attack. It's what he would have done. He tried to crouch low, to present a smaller target and to appear below where the man would be looking. He got woozy, though, and almost fell over.

He couldn't let that happen because he was dealing with the very real possibility at this point that if he fell down he'd never get up again. He took a breath and peeked around the corner.

He couldn't see anyone, so he moved as quickly as he could, gun at the ready.

The alleyway he was looking at appeared empty except for assorted dumpsters, any of which his enemy could be using to hide behind.

"Nothing we can do about it, Cindy, we're going to have to run the gauntlet," he said.

Only problem was his delusion of her wouldn't answer him back, just smile and nod at him.

"Stay behind me," he told her, even though he knew she wasn't really there. It was silly, but he had to do everything he could to stay focused, stay alive. And if that meant hallucinating that she was there, well, he was just fine with that.

"Once we kill him, there's just three more," Jeremiah said, trying to reassure himself as well as his hallucination. He stepped forward, but after three strides he could swear he felt her hand on his shoulder.

He stopped dead in his tracks. His mind was trying to tell him something, warn him somehow. He was just steps from the first dumpster. "Careful," he heard Cindy whisper in his ear.

He wanted to reassure her that he would be, but he dared not speak in that moment. He stood for a few moments, trying to listen, trying to be ready for the moment there was any sign of movement.

It was a waiting game. Normally he was very good at those. He had once waited eighteen hours for an enemy to make the first move. He'd worn them down, they'd tried to shift position slightly, that was all. And Jeremiah had killed him.

But he didn't have time to wait now. Not when he was swaying on his feet and his mind was conjuring images of his fiancée to keep him sane and awake. Depending what all was in the dumpster his bullets may or not make it through to the man hiding on the other side.

Ordinarily he would have gone low, shooting underneath the dumpster in an attempt to hit Hazim in the ankles. He couldn't get low enough to take those shots. Even if he could his hand was starting to shake and there was no guarantee that he could actually hit his target.

He could try a warning shot, see if he could successfully spook Hazim and get the man to run or at least expose himself enough to shoot back. It wasn't a great idea, but it was all he had at the moment. He lifted his gun and sent one bullet through the dumpster and another just over it.

It worked. Hazim exploded out from behind the dumpster, firing off a shot that went wild, then raced down the alley. Jeremiah aimed and fired. The bullet hit Hazim in the back of the shoulder, sending him crashing face down onto the ground. He had wanted to shoot him in the back of the head, but had had to settle for going for a body shot that he was less likely to miss with the tremors he was having.

He walked forward as fast as he could. "We're going to get him, Cindy," he muttered.

He turned around and his beautiful hallucination wasn't there. He frowned. He needed her. Maybe in the depths of his subconscious he didn't want her to have to see him kill someone, even if she was just a figment of his imagination.

It wasn't like she hadn't witnessed it before. Still, he guessed he wasn't comfortable with it. He always wanted to protect her, not just from the bad guys in the world but also from the darkness he had deep within himself.

"Sometimes good guys have to do things that most people wouldn't understand," he muttered. "Cindy gets that, don't you?"

The hallucination still didn't return.

He turned back to Hazim to see the man had regained his feet and was trying to make it to the end of the alley. Jeremiah walked after him, gun at the ready. It was better at this point to get closer so that he didn't waste another bullet on another non-killing shot.

He shuffled forward as quickly as he could, worried that he'd have to take another shot anyway to prevent Hazim from turning at the corner and disappearing from his sight.

"We'll get him, Cindy, don't worry," he said.

There was no doubt of it in his mind. Killing the other three men might prove difficult or even impossible, but this one was his, and there was no way that Jeremiah was going to let him escape.

"He should just give up," he muttered.

The man had reached the end of the alley. Jeremiah readied himself to shoot. Before he could do that, or the man could even choose which way to turn, Jeremiah's Cindy hallucination came back.

This time she was turning the corner.

"We've got him surrounded now," Jeremiah said, his words starting to really slur.

Then Hazim grabbed Cindy and locked an arm around her throat as he turned her, using her as a human shield. He put a knife to her throat.

"Stay back!" Hazim shouted.

Jeremiah smiled and kept walking forward. "Good job, Cindy, now he thinks you're real, too. We've got an advantage."

"Not another step!" Hazim screeched.

"Jeremiah!" Cindy shouted.

"Don't worry, honey, we've got him," Jeremiah said, still approaching, and taking careful aim with his gun.

Then he noticed that there was a thin trickle of blood rolling down her throat from where the tip of the knife was piercing her skin.

He gaped in horror as the truth dawned on him. This wasn't his hallucination. That was the real flesh-and-blood Cindy. And Hazim was about to kill her.

18

Cindy was terrified as a man held a knife to her throat. The blade was cutting into her skin and she could feel blood beginning to trickle out. That wasn't what was frightening her, though. Jeremiah was standing twenty feet away and he looked like a walking corpse.

His clothes were singed and tattered. His skin where she could see it was bright red, as though he had been burnt badly. The exception was the area around his eyes which instead was bone white, as if there was no blood in him. His left shoulder was jutting out at an odd angle and the arm was dangling uselessly at his side. His left hand was wrapped in bloody gauze. He held his right arm out straight, a gun gripped in his hand. But it was shaking badly, as though he couldn't bear the physical weight of keeping his arm raised.

"Jeremiah! What happened to you?" she burst out.

"I've been blown up," he said shortly.

She wanted to run to him, but the man holding her had a grip of steel and the prick of the knife reminded her that he could end her life at any moment. She wished she and Jeremiah had been able to do something about the self-defense lessons they'd discussed the week before.

"Let her go, Hazim, and come and face me," Jeremiah said, his words slightly slurred.

The man holding her rattled something off in a language she didn't recognize. She kept her eyes laser focused on

Jeremiah. He had managed to kill the Passion Week Killer in a similar situation but this time he was wounded and couldn't even hold his gun still. Instinctually she knew he wasn't going to shoot in his current state and risk hitting her.

Which meant she had to get clear of Hazim in order to give Jeremiah a fighting chance to take him down. Because of the angle at which Hazim was holding the knife she couldn't just let herself go limp and fall without risking driving the knife into her throat.

Jeremiah dropped his head slightly backward for a second. Then he took a tiny step backward with his right foot. Then he bent his right elbow and moved it backward ever so slightly before straightening it again. To Hazim it probably looked like he was getting weaker. Cindy knew better. It was a message to her.

She snapped her head back as hard as she could, slamming it into Hazim's chin. Then she stomped down on his instep with her right foot and elbowed him hard in the stomach. He dropped the knife and she sprang to the side, hitting the ground hard and skinning her good arm in the process.

Jeremiah fired twice and Hazim fell beside her, his blood running onto the ground in rivulets. She jumped up and ran to Jeremiah who was weaving on his feet.

She wanted to throw her arms around him, but realized doing so would hurt him more. She came to a stop right in front of him and as much as it killed her, she didn't touch him.

"You're alive!" she burst out.

"And you're really here," he said, his eyes clearly struggling to focus on her.

"We have to get you to the hospital."

"Not until this is done," he said. "Otherwise we'll be running for the rest of our lives."

"At least we'll *have* lives," she urged.

"I need you to go back and be safe," he said.

"I'm not leaving your side until this is done, one way or the other," she told him.

"Stubborn," he muttered.

"And don't you forget it. So, what's our next move?" she asked.

~

Something had been bothering Mark for a while about everything that was happening. Now that he was thinking along a different line, though, namely who might have it in for Cindy, then he felt like he almost had his finger on it.

"Look," he spoke up suddenly, interrupting whatever the others were talking about at that moment. "I'm sure this is all about Cindy and not Jeremiah."

"So you said, but how do you figure?" Don asked.

"Paul was suspicious about Peter's death and then Paul gets killed. Okay, I can see how reading through Paul's notes could make Keenan suspicious, but there's just nothing more he can point to on either one. If he kept digging through all the files that had to deal with Cindy and Jeremiah he could have come across the fact that there was no absolute proof that the man Jeremiah killed at the wedding was related to Joseph's stalker. So, now he's grasping at straws."

"We've established all that already," Geanie said with a frown.

"Ah! But I'm not done," Mark said, feeling excitement really starting to take hold. "Then Ben gets killed. And no one on this earth has any inkling that anyone might have a grudge against him except for-"

"Jeremiah," Joseph piped up.

"Wrong!" Mark said.

They were all taken aback by that.

"Cindy. Cindy is the one that had a very intense fight with him leading to her very publicly quitting her job. Jeremiah might not have liked him, but Cindy was the real loser in that scenario. Then the church members get on the bandwagon and make him hire Cindy back. That still doesn't mean that she likes him and that he's not trying to make her life miserable, threatening her and Jeremiah's relationship."

"But, that's ludicrous. No one would ever think of Cindy as a killer," Traci said.

"Exactly! So, when they kill the pastor they have to frame Jeremiah instead of her. It turns out to be easier than they would have thought because Detective Keenan already thinks he's a murderer. He just can't prove it. So, someone comes into contact with Keenan and manages to figure out that he already has suspicions about Jeremiah. With a little creative digging they discover that there is a piece of evidence they can plant at Jeremiah's house to implicate him in at least one murder, Paul's. They probably even leave the crumpled-up piece of paper at Ben's to make it look like he had a late-night meeting with Jeremiah. Unfortunately for them, Keenan and his people missed it."

"But who could possibly hate Cindy enough to want to hurt her or discredit Jeremiah?" Don asked.

Mark began to grin from ear-to-ear. "Someone who blames her directly for ruining their life. Someone who can justify having a pastor killed because he inadvertently assisted Cindy in ruining someone's life when he pushed her to quit her job at the church. Because after she quit her job-"

"She went to work for the Rayburn company!" Geanie blurted out.

Mark nodded. "Where she-"

"Exposed her boss as a killer," Joseph added excitedly.

"Thereby ruining-"

"It's Nita Rayburn!" Geanie screamed. "She hates Cindy. She wants her dead and she blames her for what happened to her fiancé because she's too much of an idiot to realize he is a killer."

"So, she takes away Cindy's fiancé," Traci said. "An eye for an eye."

"And, since Cindy is the best witness the prosecution has against Cartwright, if Nita could discredit her or drive her crazy then there's a chance her man won't be convicted of killing his secretary!" Mark finished triumphantly.

"It's diabolical," Don said.

"Twisted genius," Geanie muttered.

"And she might've gotten away with it," Joseph said.

"If it weren't for my amazing husband," Traci said proudly. She jumped up and gave him a huge kiss.

"But she couldn't have done this all alone," Geanie said.

"Agreed. I've met the woman. I'm inclined to believe she hired someone else to do the actual dirty work for her. So, we'll have to prove a paper trail there somewhere unless we can get a confession out of her," Mark said.

"That wasn't entirely what I was thinking," Geanie said.

Mark nodded. "You're wondering just how complicit Detective Keenan is in all this?"

The others nodded.

"Well, best case scenario is that he flapped his lips too much during the last couple weeks' investigations. The worst-case scenario is that she seduced him into helping her plant the evidence. He didn't like Jeremiah and was so convinced of his guilt that I could see him doing something stupid like that. I don't see him killing the pastor, though."

"This is all well and good, but we need to get out of here so we can start to prove this," Don said.

"I agree," Mark told him. "After Cindy's escape, though, I don't think we'll have any success trying another one."

"And they're not going to let us go until the danger is over," Geanie said.

"So, we'll just have to think of a compelling reason why it would be better if they did," Mark said.

~

As wonderful as it was to look at Cindy, Jeremiah was upset that she was in harm's way. This was exactly what he hadn't wanted to happen. That's why he'd asked Martin to watch out for her, for all of them. Now that she was here, though, he didn't dare let her out of his sight for even a minute.

"We need to get out of here before someone comes," he said.

The shots he had fired would be heard and they could be discovered at any time.

"Do you have a car?" he asked.

"No."

That was unfortunate, but they'd make do. He started walking, hating that he was so unsteady on his feet and hating even more that she had to see him this way.

"Where are we going?" she asked.

"Away."

That was about the level of thought he was capable of at the moment which was a very bad thing. He needed rest and medical treatment and the situation was growing even more dire. He couldn't stop until the remaining three terrorists were killed, though.

They turned a couple of corners in quick succession, trying to get as far from a line of sight of Hazim's body as possible. If only he knew which hotel they were all meeting at, then that would be something.

He stopped to rest, leaning against a building. Remembering the phone he'd taken from the car he pulled it out of his pocket. Hazim had been about to text something when he ran from the car. Jeremiah tried to focus on the screen, but his vision blurred, and he couldn't make out the words. He finally handed it to Cindy.

"What does it say?"

"I don't know, it's not in English," she said after a moment.

"I need someone who can read it," he muttered.

"Mind if I give it a try?"

Fortunately, Jeremiah recognized Martin's voice, so he didn't have to try and raise his weapon. He realized he was still holding the gun. He should put it away. It looked incredibly conspicuous. Then again, everything about him did right then.

He turned his head slowly as the C.I.A. agent walked up to them.

"How did you find me?" Jeremiah asked.

"How do you think? I just followed the trail of bodies," Martin said. "You know, you really aren't subtle."

"That was fast," Jeremiah said, his words slurring even more.

"And a good thing to by the looks of you," Martin said. "Time for the hospital."

"I told you no. Not until it's done," Jeremiah said.

"Well, in that case, I have good news for both of us. We think we figured out where the meeting is happening this evening."

Jeremiah nodded. "Fantastic. Take me there."

"I'd rather not. In your condition you're more of a liability than anything else."

"I have to know they're dead. I won't take anyone's word for it," Jeremiah said.

The pain was spiking so high that he was in danger of blacking out again. Every time he breathed, let alone spoke, more pain knifed through him. He probably had some cracked ribs as well. Frankly, he'd be shocked if he didn't.

"I know I'm going to regret this," Martin said. He lifted his watch to his lips. "Send in the car."

Moments later a black sedan pulled up. Jeremiah accepted Martin and Cindy's help getting into the back. They also got in with him. As soon as the door closed the driver took off.

Martin turned and looked at Cindy. "One of these days you and I are going to have a long talk," he said.

"Yeah? Well maybe that won't end up a win for you," she said.

Jeremiah wanted to chuckle. Cindy was adorable when she was defiant like this. At the moment, though, he had much more pressing urges. He was about to black out.

~

Jeremiah slumped over and Cindy gave a little scream.

"He's alive. He just blacked out," Martin said. "Which is good for us because it gives us a chance to get him to the hospital."

"No."

"What do you mean "no"?" Martin asked her incredulously.

"We're not taking him to the hospital until this is over."

"We're not playing here," he told her. "There's still a chance that even if we get him to the hospital right now that he's still going to die. He could have an infection, blood poisoning, and if he has any more blood loss-"

"I know," Cindy said, biting her lip and trying not to cry. "But he feels the need to see this through and I love him too much to rob him of that. I don't want him to spend the rest of his life looking over his shoulder."

"That's kind of the nature of our business," Martin said through gritted teeth.

"He's out of that business," Cindy said.

"Just because you're retired doesn't mean you're out. Not really. It stays with you forever even if you spend your days in a rocking chair on your front porch."

"Please. I owe him this," she said.

"For the record I think this is a terrible idea," he said.

"I understand."

"Okay. Then you might want to say a prayer."

"For Jeremiah?" she asked.

"For all of us. We're about to walk into the lion's den."

~

Two hours later Cindy's heart was pounding as she sat waiting in a hotel lobby. Everyone else in the lobby, as far as she understood it, worked for the government. Even the guy dressed as a bellboy. She was pretty certain she was the only civilian there. Even the bellboy who looked like he was all of nineteen was a spy.

Jeremiah was tucked away in a corner. He was wearing fresh clothes and his hand was now neatly bandaged, so he didn't look instantly terrifying and out of place. He was on a sofa leaning his head against the wall behind it and she couldn't tell from moment to moment whether or not he was awake or asleep.

Or alive or dead, the thought came to her unbidden.

She had a hard time believing this was about to be all over. There were so many things in her life lately that she was getting no sense of actual closure on. It was getting a bit difficult to deal with.

She nearly jumped when a couple of men came walking in through the front doors carrying briefcases. They were dressed like ordinary businessmen, but there was something about them that she didn't like. Maybe it was because she was keyed up. Maybe it was because they were in the wrong place at the wrong time. And then, when she saw Martin nod to someone out of the corner of her eye, she realized that maybe she didn't like them because they were arms dealers.

She felt her stomach twist in knots as the men took positions on chairs not that far from her. She wanted to get up and run. Part of her wanted to run out the door and not look back. The other part of her wanted to run to Jeremiah. Either way she had to fight her instincts and just sit there pretending to read the book that Martin had handed her.

The elevators opened and three men in expensive looking suits came out. They were speaking in another language, but she clearly heard them say "Hazim". Her stomach tensed even more as she realized that these were the three men Jeremiah was here to kill before they could kill him or her. Which meant, these three also knew what she looked like. She quickly buried her head in her book. Her heart was pounding so hard now that she felt like she couldn't catch her breath.

Martin had told her that they planned to capture all the men together. From where she sat she could see five agents, including Martin. She hoped that was enough. She wondered if they'd spring into action when the Iranians first greeted the arms' dealers or wait until the transaction was underway or even finished.

Martin hadn't shared details and she hadn't asked. Making sure that she and Jeremiah were here in the first place had been a fight and a half. She figured once she accomplished that she should just keep her mouth shut and not try and draw too much attention to her presence by anyone.

She should have expected what happened next, but she was certain that it caught everyone by surprise. Jeremiah, who she'd thought was unconscious, sprung to his feet and approached the three men who had come out of the elevator.

He lifted his gun and shot two of them before the third could even draw his weapon. She turned her head and saw Martin lunge to his feet with a look of panic on his face. Jeremiah and the remaining terrorist stood, facing each other.

"Still alive," Jeremiah snarled. "Can't say that for your friends. Including Hazim."

The other man looked like a trapped animal.

"Now that it's just down to us, why don't you tell me what all this is about?" Jeremiah said.

"Twelve years ago, you killed my older brother. We were all standing there, shoulder-to-shoulder. He was in the middle and you killed him. It was as though the rest of us didn't even exist. Our youngest brother was ten at the time. You killed him in the church. You never even look at the faces of those you are hurting."

"Your brother was the target, not you," Jeremiah said evenly.

"But you should have known better. You should have seen the looks of hate on our faces. But how could you?"

"Because you think I only fired straight ahead, that I never looked to the left or the right," Jeremiah said.

"You never did," the man said, his face contorting in hatred. "And you still don't."

Cindy screamed as she realized that the two arms' dealers had circled around behind Jeremiah. Martin and the agent dressed as the bellboy fired, killing both of them.

Jeremiah never even flinched. Instead he smiled. "I don't have to, because, you see, I have brothers, too."

Jeremiah fired a second before the other man. The Iranian fell, a bullet hole in the middle of his forehead. His shot grazed Jeremiah's arm.

And just like that it was all over.

Cindy gasped, clutching at her chest as she watched the tableau before her.

"I told you I wanted someone to take in alive," Martin growled.

Jeremiah turned to look at him. "And I told you that was never going to happen."

Suddenly, Jeremiah collapsed on the ground. Cindy jumped to her feet and ran over to him as Martin dropped next to him and put his fingers against Jeremiah's throat.

A second later Martin ripped open Jeremiah's shirt and started doing chest compressions.

"What's happening?" Cindy cried.

"He's gone into cardiac arrest," he said, his face grim.

"What?"

"No pulse. Someone get me an ambulance!" Martin barked.

Cindy dropped to her knees and just started to scream.

19

Wednesday dawned, and Cindy was still tired, but so much better than she had been. Everything since going to the emergency room late Monday night was a blur. Jeremiah had spent hours in surgery. After that everyone else had transitioned back to Joseph and Geanie's house and been thoroughly debriefed by Martin.

She had slept most of Tuesday but she knew that Mark had spent a lot of time on the phone with Liam sorting everything out. She had been only a little surprised to hear that they had figured out that Nita was behind framing Jeremiah. Her ill-placed love for Cartwright was going to result in her going to jail as well as him.

The doctors were planning to lift Jeremiah's medically induced coma later that night. She couldn't wait to see him and talk to him.

In the meantime, her friends had convinced her that the trip she'd originally planned to take her parents on to The Zone was a good idea. A theme park was just what the doctor had ordered for the rest of them. It was disappointing that Jeremiah wasn't there. At least Geanie, Joseph, Traci, Mark, and the kids were joining her, her parents and Kyle. She was incredibly grateful for the buffer.

Since it was Rachel, Ryan, and Kyle's first times to the park they managed to get them Rookie buttons that they could wear which let the Referees who worked there know that they were first-time visitors. They got MVP buttons for Carol and Traci since they were celebrating Mother's Day a couple of days early.

Once inside the park Traci and Mark made a beeline toward the Kids Zone to take Ryan and Rachel on some of the fairy tale inspired rides there. Kyle, as Cindy had predicted, headed straight for the Extreme Zone where they had bungee jumping, zip lining, and other high adrenaline activities.

Just as she was starting to panic Geanie squeezed her shoulder and whispered, "We're sticking with you."

Cindy gave her a grateful smile.

"So, where to?" Don asked with a grin. "The Thrill Zone, History Zone, Splash Zone, Exploration Zone?"

"We're all meeting up in the History Zone for dinner, so I suggest we do that one a little closer to then," Joseph said. "Otherwise I say we let Carol decide."

"Exploration Zone I guess," she said with a shrug.

As they explored the park Cindy noticed that while all the rest of them were doing their best to have a good time that her mom just refused to crack a smile. It was starting to grate on her nerves, but she was doing her best to keep cheerful anyway. Her parents would be flying home in a couple of days and at least she was getting to spend time with her dad who genuinely seemed to be enjoying himself.

After going on several attractions, they found themselves in the Muffin Mansion whose claim to fame was selling the largest selection of muffins anyone had ever seen. The Referee who was helping them was a tiny, blonde dynamo. Her nametag said Becca.

Cindy couldn't help but notice that Becca was hopping from foot to foot like she just couldn't keep still.

"Hmmm, I think I'd like to try the rum raisin," Don said.

"They're gone," Becca said.

"Why are the rum raisin always gone?" Geanie wailed.

Becca looked left and right then leaned forward. "Pirates," she whispered confidentially and then nodded as if to say it was all true.

"Okay," Don said. "I'll try a Peanut Butter muffin."

"Oooh, good choice," Becca said.

Joseph chose a carrot muffin while Geanie had a mixed berry.

"What on earth is a zucchini muffin?" Carol asked.

"It's like zucchini bread. It's a lot better than it sounds," Becca assured her.

Ultimately Cindy's mom opted for an orange muffin while Cindy ordered a chocolate chocolate chip muffin. Becca looked at all their muffins in such a longing way it was almost downright creepy.

At last they exited with their muffins and ate them as they strolled around. Her father in particular seemed to be really enjoying his. Even her mom, though, seemed to be pleased with her choice.

"Peanut butter muffin, who would have thought?" he asked as he finished his off.

"I'm going to have to try making these orange ones at home," Carol said.

"Sounds like a win for me," Don said.

She smiled at that which made Cindy start to relax more.

The rest of the day went well, and they were all starved by the time they made it to Aphrodite's, a beautiful restaurant in the Ancient Greece section of the History Zone.

The inside of the restaurant was beautiful and elegant with white marble and friezes all over the walls. They were quickly escorted to a large table in a private room. Once everyone had a chance to order and say what they had seen and done throughout the day Cindy nervously raised her glass of soda.

"I'd like to propose a toast."

"To another adventure survived?" Mark quipped.

Cindy laughed despite her sudden nervousness. "That, too. No, seriously, I'd like to propose a toast to two fantastic mothers. I know Mother's Day is still a couple of days away, but Mom, Traci, thank you for everything that you do."

There was a round of cheers as everyone clinked glasses. Once everyone had set them back down Cindy pulled a small jewelry box out of her purse. She glanced at Geanie who nodded encouragingly.

"Mom, I found something for you that you haven't seen in a long time. I thought you'd like to have it," Cindy said, handing her mother the box.

A look of panic flashed over Kyle's face and she realized that he had forgotten about a present. She wanted to smirk, to lord it over him as the better kid, but she couldn't. Especially not given what the nature of the gift was. Before she could think she said, "It's from both of us, Kyle and me."

Her brother flashed her a look of surprised gratitude and she smiled at him. This moment was, after all, about their mother and it didn't seem like the time to play one-upmanship with him.

"Happy Mother's Day, Mom," he said hastily.

Carol beamed and looked genuinely happy as she held the box in her hands. "I wonder what it could be," she said.

"Open it and find out," Don urged.

Carol opened the box. Inside was the locket that Geanie had helped Cindy find while going through the box of jewelry she had rescued from Lisa's room when she was a kid. The gold locket had a picture of Lisa and another one of Kyle.

Carol picked it up and her face turned ashen. "What is this?" she asked.

"It's the locket you gave Lisa on her tenth birthday. The one you glued Kyle's picture in, so she couldn't look at any other boys, remember?" Cindy said with a smile.

The locket war had lasted nearly a year and had been funny to watch. Cindy was hoping it would bring as many good memories to her mom as seeing it had to her.

"Wow, I remember..." Kyle started. "That is, it was all pretty funny. She loved that locket," he said, backpedaling so as not to seem like he hadn't known that was what was in the box.

Carol turned to Kyle. "You knew about this?" she asked.

He hesitated for a moment and then nodded. As she continued to stare at him his smile started to fade. Finally, Carol turned to Cindy. She narrowed her eyes.

"How dare you?" she hissed.

"Excuse me?" Cindy asked, taken aback.

"You kept this behind my back?" Carol demanded, shaking her fist with the locket dangling from it. "I ordered all of her junk destroyed."

"Carol, it's a thoughtful gesture," Don said.

"Right up there with burying a dagger in my heart," Carol said.

She threw the locket at Cindy. "Treacherous traitor. I always knew you had it in for me, but I would have thought this was beyond even you."

Cindy stared, gaping, as she tried to comprehend how this had gone so badly.

"Mom-" Kyle tried to intervene.

"Shut up. Don't try and take the blame for your sister. I know you weren't stupid enough to know what was in that box."

Kyle went completely pale at that.

"Carol, it's time you let it go," Don said, his voice firm.

"Let it go?" she raged. "Our baby girl died, and it was all Cindy's fault, and you want me to let it go?"

Cindy felt like she'd been slapped in the face. "How dare you blame me for what happened to Lisa? It was her fault. She was the one who forced Kyle and me up there with her taunting and bullying. There is no one to blame for Lisa's death but Lisa. And after all these years I'm trying to remember the good parts of her life, the times we had fun together. Which isn't always easy given that you don't want to even acknowledge that she existed most of the time!"

"It hurts too much."

"That's life. You don't think I wasn't hurt, damaged for years? You think you lost a lot? The day she died I lost my sister and my mother."

"You ungrateful little disappointment. You can never make it up to me for her loss. Not ever. I wish you'd died instead of her!"

Carol stormed out of the restaurant and the rest of them just sat there in shock. After a few seconds Joseph asked, "Is someone going to go after her?"

"Nope," Don said, picking up his water and taking a sip.

Kyle looked even more stricken than Cindy felt. He looked up at Cindy and there was horror in his eyes. Suddenly he looked to her exactly like he'd looked on that terrible day so many years before. There was the same shock and fear and confusion on his face.

"Cindy?" he asked, lips trembling. "I'd like the locket," he said.

She handed it to him and he opened it up and stared at the two pictures inside. Tears began to stream down his cheeks. He looked back up at her.

"Thank you. This is the best gift anyone could have received."

"Mom doesn't agree," she said, struggling not to cry.

"Mom's wrong. About a lot of things," he said, whispering at the end.

"Thank you."

"You're stronger and braver than I could ever be. And you're so much more than Lisa was, too. You're the best of us and I'm sorry I haven't told you that before," he said.

She got up from her seat, walked over and hugged her brother. He wrapped his arms around her and buried his head in her shoulder as they both began to cry.

"I've worked so hard to try and get her approval," Kyle said. "Not anymore. She doesn't deserve my effort or yours."

"No, she doesn't," Cindy said, choking a bit on the words.

"I'm sorry I've been so stupid and so selfish. I'm sorry I didn't understand you. I don't like Jeremiah, but I am grateful that he's made you so happy and I'll never say a bad thing about him again," he vowed.

Cindy cried harder and hugged Kyle tighter. "Thank you," she whispered.

At last she let go of her brother and went back to her seat. She noticed that everyone at the table seemed to be struggling with their emotions. Everyone except her father. He looked up at her, his face a mask.

"I'm sorry. I thought I could help her, but I can't. She's refused therapy. Over the years I kind of gave up. I figured she was just who she was at this point. But what she just said is completely unacceptable. I love you, Cindy. I love you, too, Kyle. And I owe it to the two of you to give it one last try to get her to a place of healing. But I promise you this. If I can't she won't step foot at your wedding."

"Thank you, Dad," Cindy said, struggling to control her emotions.

"We don't need her there," Kyle said, his voice strong. "Anything you need for the wedding, Cindy, and I'll do everything I can to get it for you."

She wiped at her eyes. "We could use a good photographer."

He smiled at her. "Done. I'll take care of that. Don't give it a second thought."

She nodded.

"Anything else, you tell me."

"Me, too," her father said.

"And us," Geanie spoke up.

"Heck, you know we've got your back," Mark said.

She looked around. "Then that's all I need."

~

After they left the theme park everyone scattered. Cindy's father went to find her mom and then was going to go straight to the airport, so they could fly home early. Joseph and Geanie went home to take care of the dogs and her Blackie. Mark and Traci took the twins home.

To her surprise Kyle offered to go with her to the hospital. She decided not to look a gift horse in the mouth. They drove to the hospital in relative silence.

Right before they got there Kyle said, "I'm sorry about Mom."

"It's not your fault."

"I feel like it is. I worked so hard to get her attention, to make her proud, that I never really realized how she was treating you."

"I seriously doubt that it would have changed anything if you hadn't worked hard to make her proud," Cindy said, trying to reassure him.

"Thank you for giving me the locket. I will treasure it."

"Now you have two things of Lisa's," she said.

"Yes. I wish I had more."

"Mom's a psycho," Cindy said.

"Yes, yes she is."

~

Jeremiah felt pain as he began to wake up. He didn't like it, but he could swear he heard Cindy's voice and more than anything he wanted to see her. Being able to see her would be worth any pain he could experience.

The pain grew sharper as he struggled to open his eyes. He became aware of other sounds around him, mostly beeping machines. He finally forced his eyes opened.

He looked up and saw Kyle smiling down at him. "There's my future brother-in-law. Glad to see you awake finally."

Jeremiah blinked rapidly, sure that this was a dream or an hallucination. Every time his eyes opened, though, Kyle was still there.

"Where am I?" Jeremiah finally asked. "Am I dead?"

"Very much the opposite," Kyle said, still smiling.

Jeremiah turned his head slowly, looking for Cindy. He had been so certain that he'd heard her voice.

"She ran to the coffee machine, she'll be right back," Kyle reassured him.

"I must be dying if you're smiling," Jeremiah said, slurring his words.

"No. You're going to live," Kyle said.

The change in Cindy's brother was bewildering to say the least. Before he could question it further Cindy walked into the room. She saw him, squealed, and set down the two cups of coffee she was holding.

She ran over to him and took his right hand in hers.

"Hey, Hon," he managed to say.

Kyle picked up one of the coffee cups. "I'll leave you two lovebirds alone for a few minutes," he said, heading out the door.

"What's with him?" Jeremiah asked.

"I'll explain later. Right now, I'm just so happy that you're okay," she gushed.

"Am I? Okay?" he asked.

"You're going to be just fine. The doctors say there will be a lot of physical therapy after your collarbone heals. The burns aren't permanently disfiguring."

"And my hand?" he asked.

She smiled. "They were able to reattach your fingers. Martin had put them on ice and we got you into an operating room with minutes to spare. The doctors say it's going to take a lot of physical therapy, but they're optimistic that in a year or so you'll regain some use of them."

"No permanent damage done," he said, relief flooding through him.

"Hopefully not."

"I'll have to thank Martin."

"We need to invite him to the wedding," Cindy said.

He chuckled at that. "Fortunately, he has time to work out his schedule. And I have time to work out my fingers," he said.

She teared up. "That's good. I want you to be able to feel it when I put a wedding ring on the one."

He grabbed the back of her head with his good hand. "Even though it's not there I feel it already," he said.

He pulled her down and kissed her. When he finally let go she pulled back and just stared at him. "I notice you waited to say something that romantic until you were in a public place and I couldn't take advantage of you," she said.

He laughed out loud. "That was not intentional."

She narrowed her eyes. "Even still, I think all of us have been spending entirely too much time in hospitals."

"Tell you what, I promise to go at least six months without getting hurt if you do."

"It's a deal."

~

Friday morning Mark walked into the police station. It hadn't even been a full week since he was there last, but it might as well have been from the way he was feeling. He made it to his desk and Liam looked up from his.

"What did I miss?" Mark asked.

Liam raised an eyebrow. "Well, you know Keenan resigned and we arrested Nita Rayburn."

It seemed anti-climactic for Mark since he hadn't been the one to arrest Nita and he hadn't seen Keenan resign. He wished he'd seen the look on the man's smug face when he realized how Nita had manipulated him into helping her with her scheme.

"Any luck yet on figuring out who Nita hired to kill the pastor and plant the evidence?"

"Unfortunately, not yet. She never knew his name, never saw a face, you know."

"Great," Mark muttered.

"Maybe the District Attorney can get it out of her, make it part of a plea deal."

Mark shook his head. "Anything else?"

"Other than that, the only things you missed around here were the discovery of a new arsonist, an off-duty officer getting the crap kicked out of him by a troop of girl scouts, and the captain almost quitting after a very heated discussion with some government type."

"What?" Mark asked, his eyes bugging out of his head.

"Yup and the Escape! Chanel is going to film a reality series here in the precinct."

"Okay, I see. You're messing with me."

"Only about the reality series. The rest happened."

"I'm out of it for a couple of days and the whole station falls apart," Mark said.

"Apparently there is no Pine Springs Police Department without you."

"Ha ha, very funny."

"It wouldn't be nearly as funny if it didn't seem true. While you were away you got about five thousand messages. They're all on your desk just waiting for you to give them your personal touch."

"You're in an interesting mood," Mark noted.

Liam flushed. "Rebecca's folks are coming into town. We're going to have dinner."

"Meeting the parents so soon?" Mark asked. "I'm shocked. One would think that you had designs on their daughter."

Liam blushed harder.

"I bet she likes it when you blush like that," Mark said. "Personally, I think it makes you look like a little school girl."

"This school girl would be happy to have it out with you," Liam said.

"Pistols at dawn? Swords at noon? I have to warn you, I'm getting quite good at dueling with spoons."

"Looks like I'm not the only one in a very special mood," he noted.

Mark smiled. "What can I say? It's a beautiful day. You've got to enjoy those while you can."

"Amen to that."

Mark took off his jacket and then sat down at his desk. He eyed the rather formidable pile of paperwork stacked there. Next to it was the pile of messages that Liam had referenced. Mark began to sift through them.

Sadie Colbert, the mother of Not Paul's son, had called. That was right. She had wanted to tell him something. He kept flipping through his messages until he came to one from Kendra in Protective Services. She was the one he'd asked to find Not Paul's son in the system. He stared at it as his stomach did a somersault. The message was marked Urgent.

20

Mark grabbed the phone and called Kendra. She answered on the third ring.

"Hi, Kendra, it's Mark Walters."

"Mark, you caught me just before I was going to lunch."

"Did you find something on the baby boy?"

There was a long pause and then she said. "You know, it's been forever since you and I had lunch. I think that's a great idea."

Alarm bells went off in his head. They'd never had lunch together. Never even met face-to-face. Something was wrong, and she clearly didn't want her coworkers overhearing her.

"Just tell me where," he said.

"The Thai Kitchen in the Old Town section of River City."

"It will take me about thirty minutes, but I'll be there."

"See you soon," she said, sounding way too chipper.

Mark hung up the phone and grabbed his jacket.

"Everything okay?" Liam asked, looking up at him with a frown.

"I don't know."

"You need backup?"

Mark shook his head. "I think I need to go alone on this." Something twisted in his stomach. He didn't like this. The last thing that had to do with his ex-partner got him stabbed and nearly killed. The knife wound was still healing, and it twinged in pain as he thought about it.

He wrote down the name of the place where he was going and handed it to Liam.

"What's this?"

"Where I'm going to meet Kendra from Protective Services for lunch right now. Call me in an hour-and-a-half and if I don't answer, send the cavalry."

"Seriously?" Liam asked.

"Yeah. Something's wrong and she clearly didn't want to say anything over the phone."

Liam nodded. "Okay. Be careful."

"You don't have to tell me twice," Mark said.

~

Cindy slipped into a pew next to Geanie and Joseph. She gave them both a nod before turning her eyes back forward. She felt so odd. She was grateful that she and all her loved ones were alive. She couldn't stop thanking God for sparing Jeremiah and for the good news she'd just had from the doctors.

Her heart was full of thanksgiving which was why she felt so out of place among the mourners. Pastor Ben's funeral was being held at the church as was fitting.

Dave was the one speaking. He was obviously very shaken up, but he was doing his best to keep it together. Her heart went out to him. He'd had it rough lately.

Geanie grabbed her hand and squeezed it. "Everything okay?" she whispered.

Cindy nodded. "We're not dead. Everything's great." It sounded horrible, but it was the truth.

Geanie smiled at her and squeezed her hand again. Warmth flooded through Cindy. It was good to have family.

~

Jeremiah was dozing when he heard a light step enter his room. He wrestled himself awake just in time to see Martin sitting down in the chair next to his hospital bed.

"Glad to see you in one piece instead of three," Martin said.

"Glad to be in one piece," Jeremiah said. "Thank you for that. I heard you saved my life, so thanks for that as well."

"Which time?" he smirked.

"Chest compressions."

"Oh that. No big deal," Martin said with a shrug.

"Don't take this the wrong way, but why are you here?"

Martin rolled his eyes. "Just a social call, I assure you. Wanted to see for myself that you really do have nine lives."

"Did you find what you were looking for after the other day?"

Jeremiah was referring to the weapon that the Iranians had planned to buy off the arms dealers.

"You mean the object that was the subject of the little business deal that you stepped in the middle of?"

Jeremiah nodded.

"We did."

"That's good."

"Of course, things could have gone smoother if you'd stuck to my plan."

"I couldn't risk any of them getting away."

"I know," Martin said grudgingly. He glanced at his watch and then stood up. "I have a plane to catch."

"Making the world a safer place?"

"Something like that. After all, I don't have to worry about Pine Springs. You've got this place covered," Martin said with a wink.

"Good luck."

"Thanks. You know, that's quite a family you've built for yourself. I wasn't sure if I should shoot some of them or recruit them."

Jeremiah chucked. "I know the feeling."

~

Mark made it to the restaurant and walked inside, scanning every face in the room. A slender woman in her forties with dark skin and short, black hair waved to him. He moved to her table.

"Kendra?" he asked.

"Mark, have a seat," she said.

"How did you know it was me?" he asked.

"You're the only guy who's come in here in the last fifteen minutes who looked like a cop."

"Seriously?"

"Yes. But I also had an advantage. I looked you up online while I was waiting."

"Don't believe everything you read," he said, not even wanting to imagine what she might have read about him online.

"So, you're not the hero cop who thwarted the Passion Week Killer?" she asked.

"I had help."

She nodded. "I ordered the ginger duck for you. It's the only good thing on the menu."

"Thanks, I think," he said.

"It should be out in a couple of minutes."

"Great. In the meantime, care to tell me why we're meeting like this?"

She dropped her eyes and picked up her water glass to take a sip. He noticed that her hand shook slightly.

"Someone hacked my home computer and my work computer yesterday," she said.

"Both? That doesn't seem like a coincidence."

"I didn't think so either. And for the last few days I've felt like someone is watching me."

"Have you talked to the police?" he asked.

She looked up at him. "That's what I'm doing right now."

"Ah, I see."

"I caught one of the supervisors looking over the files in my inbox two days ago when I got back from lunch early. He tried to pass it off that he thought I had a file he needed, but…"

"But something felt wrong about it?" Mark guessed.

She nodded.

"So, when did all this weirdness start?" he asked.

"That's just it. It started the day after you called and asked me to look for a baby surrendered at a police station near UCLA thirteen years ago."

Mark stared at her. "You don't think it's related, do you?"

She leaned forward. "I've been in this job for seventeen years and nothing like what's happened the last few days has ever happened to me before. You tell me."

"It can't be," Mark said, not wanting to believe. "I mean, that's impossible."

"You said this was part of an active investigation."

He nodded. "It is."

That was sort of true. It was an active investigation of his even if it was not officially on the books at work.

"So, I'm asking you what you've gotten me mixed up in?"

"Honestly, I'm not sure. It shouldn't have led to what you're describing."

"Well, I've got two kids of my own, and I've decided this would be a fine time for us all to go visit my folks in Atlanta."

"Okay."

The food arrived, and Mark waited until the waitress had left before resuming the conversation.

"If you want me to investigate what's happening-"

She shook her head fiercely. "I don't want any more part of whatever this is. I've dealt with deadbeat parents, junkies, psychotic kids, and things most people can't even imagine in this job. But I have never before worried for my personal safety."

He tried to tell himself that she was imagining things, but deep down he had a sick feeling that wouldn't go away. They ate their lunch quickly with few words exchanged as Mark thought over what she was saying. When the check came he paid for her lunch. It seemed the least he could do under the circumstances.

He finally addressed the one thing they hadn't discussed. "Did you find the kid?" he asked.

She stared at him and a muscle in her jaw twitched. "I've been debating for the last twenty minutes whether or not I should tell you, whether it would help you or just make things worse for everyone."

He was stunned that she was actively considering holding out on him.

"This is an active investigation and as such-"

She held up her hand. "Save it. This isn't about who's entitled to what information. This is bigger than that. So, until whatever this is goes away, I don't expect to hear from you again."

She stood abruptly and lifted her purse off the table. Underneath it was an envelope. She met his eyes, nodded almost imperceptibly and then walked out.

Mark reached out and slid the envelope over and swiftly put it inside his jacket. He felt like every eye in the room was on him, though in truth he couldn't see anyone looking his way. He couldn't help but wonder if this was how Jeremiah had felt during his days as a spy.

Mark stood up and made his way quickly to his car. Once inside he started the engine and drove off. He wanted to delay for a minute, so he could review the contents of the envelope, but Kendra had spooked him too badly. It almost felt like his skin was crawling as he imagined people watching him, too.

"Stop being paranoid," he muttered to himself.

It didn't do much good as he found himself speeding down the highway trying to get away from there as quickly as possible. He decided Jeremiah had to have been cooler headed about this sort of thing otherwise the man would have dropped dead of a heart attack years before.

He was almost back at the precinct when his phone rang startling him badly. It was Liam.

"I'm fine," he said, answering his phone.

"Glad to hear someone is."

"What's wrong?" Mark asked quickly.

"Sadie Colbert stopped by looking for you. She seemed very agitated and wouldn't talk to anyone else. She just left here a couple of minutes ago."

"Do you know where she was heading?"

"She said you could reach her at home."

"Okay, I'm going to head over there," Mark said.

"Alright. Everything go okay?"

"Yeah, I think so. Just weird."

"You'll have to tell me about it."

"I will," Mark promised.

He got off the freeway an exit early and a few minutes later he parked outside Sadie's house. He sat there for a minute trying to collect himself. He pulled the envelope out of his jacket and slowly opened it. Inside he found a piece of paper and a picture of a thirteen-year-old boy. He looked so much like Not Paul that it gave Mark a start. He sat staring at the picture feeling like he was looking at a ghost.

He finally tore his eyes away from it and looked at the piece of paper. There was an address in Los Angeles and a name. Darren Bradley Michaelson. He carefully folded the paper and put it back into the envelope. Then he put the envelope and the photo in his jacket pocket. He sat for another minute, trying to gather his composure.

So many emotions were rushing through him. "He looks like a fine boy, Paul," he said. He wished his former partner could hear him.

"That's it, too many emotional days this week," he said, struggling to pull it together. "Enough of those."

He got out of the car and went up to the front door. As soon as he rang the bell the door flew open and Sadie stood there, eyes wide, cheeks tear-stained.

"Are you okay?" he asked in alarm.

She shook her head and turned away. Mark walked in and shut the front door behind him. He followed her into the living room and sat down on the couch while she took a seat in an armchair.

If anything, the room looked even more dilapidated than it had when he was first there which hadn't been that many days earlier. Sadie herself looked like a complete and utter wreck.

She covered her face with her hands and then suddenly took them down and leaned forward. "Do you see me? Do you really see *me*?" she asked.

"Um-"

"Of course you don't," she interrupted. "How could you because I haven't told you. You don't see *me*. You see *her*."

He tried to think of a tactful way of asking if she was on any medication or, perhaps, off of it. She hadn't been like this when they first met, and he was wondering what exactly had changed.

"What's wrong, Sadie?" he asked.

She laughed like he'd just said the funniest thing in the whole world. "That. That's what's wrong, right there," she said.

"I'm sorry. I'm not following you."

"I have a secret," she said, leaning close as though she didn't want anyone else to overhear. Given that she lived alone it was creepy and he had just about had his fill of creepy for the day.

"What is it?" he asked.

She started to speak, then stopped. She tried again and stopped again. Tears came to her eyes. "Why is it so hard to admit? After all these years. It doesn't matter now. My parents are gone. Paul is gone. There's no one to care."

"You can tell me what it is," Mark said.

She nodded and took a deep breath. It was as though he could watch her actually pull herself together, like her sanity was a threadbare shawl that she was trying to wrap around her soul.

"I'm not Sadie Colbert," she said.

Mark had not been expecting that. "Who are you?" he asked.

"I'm Sandra. Sandra Colbert."

And suddenly her whole body relaxed, and she gave him a tentative smile. "You don't know how good it feels to say that," she told him.

"I thought Sandra was kidnapped by the cult," he said.

She shook her head. "That's what everyone thought, but it was Sadie that they grabbed. Not me. I'm Sandra."

"I don't understand," he said.

She nodded and reached out and patted his knee. "Let me explain. Sadie and I were twins. When we were little we'd play pranks on our babysitters and even our parents by switching identities."

"How very *Parent Trap*," he said, thinking of the old Disney film.

"For some reason we always thought it was funny to trick people into calling us the wrong name. Well, when they kidnapped Sadie, she was pretending to be me."

"Once your parents knew what had happened, why didn't you tell them?" he asked, wondering how something like that ended up becoming a decades long secret.

A tear trickled down her cheek. "I was going to, but my parents were beside themselves with grief. And they said something that parents should never say."

"What?" Mark asked.

"They said that if they had to lose one of their children they were glad it worked out this way because they always liked Sadie best."

Mark thought of Ryan and Rachel and he felt sick to the bottom of his soul. He could never imagine preferring one to the other let alone saying it out loud.

"Oh, dear heavens," he whispered.

She nodded. "When I heard that I felt that I couldn't make it worse by telling them the truth, that Sadie, their favorite, was the one who was taken. So, I just kept being her."

"I'm so sorry," Mark said, realizing that it explained a lot about how she had gotten as messed up as she was.

"It was terrible, but I had resigned myself to being Sadie. Then… then I met Paul."

"Oh no," Mark whispered, starting to see.

She nodded. "And he had known Sadie, the real Sadie, in the cultists' camp. He knew I was lying. He'd heard my name and came to find me and knew straight away that I was really Sandra. And he said my name. And no one had said my name in so many years. And he understood my pain."

"And the two of you ended up in a relationship," Mark finished.

She nodded. "My whole life he was the only person who ever knew the truth."

Mark took her hand. "It's time to step into the light, Sandra," he said gently.

A little sob escaped her, but then she smiled at him. She was going to need a lot of counseling, but maybe there was hope for her to live a normal life in the future. He hoped so.

"When I found out Paul was dead, I realized there wasn't anyone left in the world who knew, and I found that unbearable. That's why I had to talk to you. I knew you'd understand."

He understood all too well. Given that Paul had also taken on the identity of another child and spent his life lying he could see how he would be attracted to Sandra who was harboring a similar secret.

"I found something I'd like to share with you," he said.

"What?" she asked, wiping at her eyes.

He pulled the picture out of his jacket and handed it to her. "His name is Darren." He knew he shouldn't have told her even that much, but he hoped it would help her in some way.

"He looks just like Paul," she said, in a slightly awed voice.

"I noticed that, too. Except he has your eyes."

"He does!" She kissed the photograph tenderly. "Thank you," she whispered.

"Happy Mother's Day."

"This means so much."

He nodded, trying to fight back his own tears. He wouldn't have understood the look on her face before he became a parent. Now, he couldn't imagine what she was going through. He couldn't even let himself think about how he would feel if strangers were raising his children.

He cleared his throat. "Do you know a counselor you can speak to?" he asked.

She nodded. "I'll find one." When she looked up at him again her eyes were clear, and she looked ten years younger. "It's time to start living again," she said. "And who knows? Maybe one day I'll get to meet my son."

"I hope so," he said.

She stood, and he rose as well. She held out her hand. "Thank you, Detective. You don't know what you've done for me."

He shook her hand solemnly. "I'm happy I could help in some small way. And thank you for sharing your story with me, Sandra."

She nodded, smiling.

The cult leader that had been Not Paul's father had destroyed so many lives. Mark was just grateful that this was one life that he could help save. Looking at her he truly did believe that she was going to get better. He smiled. It was a new day in so many ways.

She walked him to the door and stood on the porch as he walked to his car. The sun was hitting her face and it seemed like it was driving away all the shadows. He smiled to himself as he unlocked his car and opened the door.

Suddenly a shot rang out. Mark hit the ground. He drew his gun and looked around, but could see no one in the street. There was no second shot and he slowly eased to a crouched position. The shot had sounded like it came from a distance. Maybe it had been a street or two over. He would call it in.

"Better get inside!" he shouted to Sandra.

She didn't say anything. She'd probably already done so like any normal person would. He turned just to make sure and his heart stopped when he saw her lying on the porch. He stood and looked around, gun extended in front of him, but there was no one anywhere that he could see. He edged his way over to the porch.

"Sandra, are you okay?" he asked, still looking for the shooter.

There was still no answer.

Finally, he was standing over her and he looked down. She was staring up at him, her lips parted slightly and eyes wide open. There was a hole right in between them.

Sandra Colbert, the mother of Not Paul's son, was dead.

Look for

ANNOINTEST MY HEAD WITH OIL

Coming Summer 2018

Debbie Viguié is the New York Times Bestselling author of more than fifty novels including the *Wicked* series, the *Crusade* series and the *Wolf Springs Chronicles* series co-authored with Nancy Holder. Debbie also writes thrillers including *The Psalm 23 Mysteries,* the *Kiss* trilogy, and the *Witch Hunt* trilogy. When Debbie isn't busy writing she enjoys spending time with her husband, Scott, visiting theme parks. They live in Florida with their cat, Schrödinger.

CPSIA information can be obtained
at www.ICGtesting.com
Printed in the USA
LVHW091534130219
607425LV00002B/322/P